DESTINY

THE MCBRIDE CHRONICLES
BOOK TWO

DESTINY

THE McBRIDE CHRONICLES
BOOK TWO

*"It's not in the stars to hold
Our destiny but in ourselves."*

WILLIAM SHAKESPEARE.
(1564-1616)

*"A person often meets his destiny on
the road he took to avoid it."*

JEAN DE LA FONTAINE
(1621-1695)

VALERIE GREEN

a novel

THE MCBRIDE CHRONICLES
BOOK TWO

hancock house

Cataloguing data available from Library and Archives Canada

978-0-88839-764-5 [paperback]

978-0-88839-765-2 [epub]

FRONT/BACK COVER DESIGN: J. RADE

FRONT COVER ARTWORK: Shutterstock

PRODUCTION & DESIGN: J. Rade, M. Lamont

EDITOR: D. MARTENS

We acknowledge the support of the Government of Canada through the Canada Book Fund and the Canada Council for the Arts, and of the Province of British Columbia through the British Columbia Arts Council and the Book Publishing Tax Credit.

Hancock House gratefully acknowledges the Halkomelem Speaking Peoples whose unceded, shared and asserted traditional territories our offices reside upon.

Published simultaneously in Canada and the United States by

HANCOCK HOUSE PUBLISHERS LTD.

19313 Zero Avenue, Surrey, B.C. Canada V3Z 9R9

#104-4550 Birch Bay-Lynden Rd, Blaine, WA, U.S.A. 98230-9436

(800) 938-1114   Fax (800) 983-2262

www.hancockhouse.com   info@hancockhouse.com

*For my amazing daughter Kate who followed her dream to find
Her destiny;
With an abundance of love.*

AUTHOR'S NOTE

Destiny (Book Two) is the story of another strong woman in the McBride family—Sarah—Jane and Gideon's rebellious daughter, who had already begun to show her fiery spirit at the end of *Providence*.

Sarah's childhood is blissful but in the process of trying to become a "respectable young woman of her era" she must experience many horrors and tragedies during her lifetime in Victoria, British Columbia—including the collapse of the Point Ellice Bridge and an unimaginably, heart-breaking love story which changes the course of her life. But, like her mother before her, she learns how to cope with the destiny that is hers.

I hope you enjoy reading *Destiny* as much as I have enjoyed writing it, and will want to read more about the McBride family in the next books, *Legacy* and *Tomorrow*.

Valerie Green, 2023

TABLE OF CONTENTS

THE McBRIDE FAMILY TREE

Angus McBride   –m–   Sarah Fraser
b.1805   b.1807
m.1829   m.1829
d.1848   d. 1856

Duncan	Gideon	Janet	Fiona
b.1830	b.1835	b.1838	b.1840
d.1848	m.1863	m.1855	m.1856
	Jane Hopkins	Tom Ritchie	Robbie Buchan

Caleb	Sarah	Albert (twin)	Edward (twin)
b.1866	b.1871	b.1872	b.1872
d.1869	m.1896	m. 1896	m.1895
	Ernest	(Antoinette	(Margaret
	Hamilton	Harris)	Bowers)

Stephen	Caleb
b.1897	b.1910

THE CALDWELL FAMILY TREE

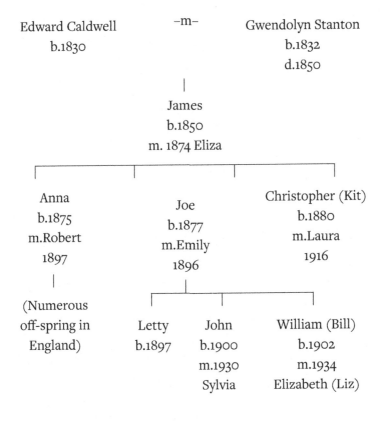

Edward Caldwell   –m–   Gwendolyn Stanton
b.1830   b.1832
                               d.1850

James
b.1850
m. 1874 Eliza

Anna	Joe	Christopher (Kit)
b.1875	b.1877	b.1880
m.Robert	m.Emily	m.Laura
1897	1896	1916

(Numerous off-spring in England)

Letty	John	William (Bill)
b.1897	b.1900	b.1902
	m.1930	m.1934
	Sylvia	Elizabeth (Liz)

PART ONE

Growing Up

SARAH
(1877-1897)

CHAPTER 1

I love our grandfather clock. It has become a large part of my life.

It stands in the grand hall foyer of our house beside the door leading to Papa's library, where it chimes out the hours of our lives in a wise, grandfatherly fashion.

DING DONG DING DONG!

One day, as I lay on my stomach on the upstairs landing of Providence looking down at the clock, I was daydreaming as usual. Well hidden behind a large pillar, lying in my very favourite place in the whole house, I was trying to listen to Papa and a visitor talking business in the library. The door was slightly ajar, and as I peered through the banister rails, I thought I might hear something interesting.

But then the clock began chiming twelve o'clock, so I could no longer clearly hear the voices. This was most annoying, because I loved eavesdropping on other people's conversations. Sometimes I even heard things not meant for my curious six-year-old ears.

I adored our house and especially the large staircase leading to the upper landing, which then divided off into two directions, with my mother's portrait on the wall in the middle. My father, Captain Gideon McBride, told me the staircase was made from California redwood trees. It had an interesting smell; a heady fragrance combined with the furniture polish our Chinese houseboy, Ah Foo, purchased in Chinatown. Mother said it was mysterious and held all the puzzling qualities of the Orient. I didn't know what that meant, but I believed her.

Once the clock had chimed twelve times, Ah Foo sounded the gong for lunch. He did the same thing at seven o'clock every night for dinner and for breakfast at eight o'clock every morning. I was about to stand up when my mother's voice startled me from behind. I jumped because I had thought she was already downstairs.

"If you keep eavesdropping, Sarah," she said, "you will hear something that you regret one day. Now, run along to your room, wash your hands and come down to the dining room at once. Didn't you hear Ah Foo sounding the gong?"

How could I not hear? It was so loud!

My mother was always reprimanding me. She was very strict. "Yes, Mother," I said obediently as she went downstairs ahead of me.

I slunk away, regretting she had found me, because I might still have heard something interesting coming from Papa's library.

I ran to my bedroom and washed my hands and face in the basin's warm water. My thoughts were still on my secret place on the stairs, though, and all the other times I had been there behind the pillar when I was supposed to be tucked up in bed sound asleep before my parents left for a dinner party or a fancy ball. Instead, I would creep out from my bedroom and lie there watching them leave. Papa always looked so handsome in his captain's uniform, and mother looked beautiful in one of her elegant gowns and wearing her sparkly jewelry. They were such an elegant couple.

The house we lived in was a mansion, and we had many servants to wait on us. We had large grounds where I could run and play, and, for my recent sixth birthday, Papa had bought me my very own pony that I named Jake. Papa and Foo were going to teach me to ride Jake once the weather improved. We also had two dogs named Cain and Abel. Mother always chose biblical names for our animals, although she hoped the dogs would not meet the same fate as their namesakes. She even insisted on calling my pony Jacob for some reason, but I preferred Jake.

I never tired of hearing Papa's tales about his adventures at sea, but Mother never spoke of her past and was quite different. She was always trying to be so proper, telling me to act like a young lady and insisting that I curb my high spirits. Most of the time, like today, I resented her for that.

I did love her, though, but in a different way than I loved Papa. It was so easy to throw myself up into his arms and hug him or jump up on his back and be taken around the garden in a piggy-back ride. He would run in the garden with me or laugh at my silly pranks. Mother would not tolerate such frivolity and would only allow a small kiss on the cheek from me. She rarely hugged me.

She spent a lot of time playing the piano which she said soothed her, or doing her charity work with a group of other rich ladies. I often watched her walking up the hill to the church to visit my little brother's grave. He had died some years before I was born. She never spoke of him, but when I asked Papa about him he said Caleb had died of smallpox fever when he was only two years old. I felt sad for Caleb up in heaven, but I sometimes felt even sadder for me here on earth, because I soon came to believe that his death had made my mother quite unable to love me.

I envied Caleb lying peacefully in his little grave on the hill, because Mother often sat there with him and sometimes planted a kiss on his tombstone. I wished I was lying there beside him, so that she would sit with me and kiss me. On Sundays, when we went to church as a family, we always took flowers to Caleb's grave.

Now, as I dried my hands, I could hear Angelina, our Portuguese nanny, hustling my annoying little twin brothers, Teddy and Bertie, downstairs. They were just over a year younger than me and had been playing in the nursery. I love Angelina because she always sings to us and cuddles us to her large bosom every night after she reads us a story.

I stopped daydreaming and ran down the stairs to join the family in the dining room. Mother was seated at one end of the long dining table. She glared at me as I came in.

"It's about time you joined us, Sarah. We are all waiting to say grace," she said.

Papa just winked at me.

* * *

After lunch, I returned to my bedroom and once again my thoughts wandered.

I began reminiscing about my Uncle James Caldwell's wedding to Aunt Eliza at St. Luke's Church when I was three. I was their flower girl, and I'd worn a white chiffon dress with a poke bonnet trimmed in lace. The dress still hung in my cupboard.

My mother had told me then: "That bonnet will cover your wild array of auburn curls and keep them in place for a change." She said it as though my curls were a curse.

Their wedding reception was held on the lawns of Providence, and Aunt Eliza looked like a fairy princess in her gown of white crepe de chine. Afterwards she gave me one of the roses from her bouquet and helped me press it in my Bible. I opened my Bible now and found the rose inside, which I fingered as the memories of that day, came rushing back.

A short time after that event, when I was lying in my secret place on the landing one day, I had overheard Mother and Papa saying that Uncle James and Aunt Eliza were expecting a baby in a few months and Uncle Edward would become a grandfather. They all seemed very happy about that. However, when I first saw Anna, their baby, and heard her screeching as babies tend to do, I didn't see what all the fuss was about. She was just another baby. I had enough trouble already with Teddy and Bertie.

While I sat daydreaming, I heard Mother on the landing, calling to Angelina.

"The men are here to install the new water closets, Angelina. Please take all the children outside to play, as there will be dust everywhere."

Goodness, what a fuss she was making as she ran up and down the corridor giving out her orders.

"This is a wonderful invention," she said to no one in particular. "It will save Foo and the maids having to carry water upstairs for our baths, or carry our chamber pots downstairs to dispose of their contents."

As she entered my room, she said, "Come, Sarah, hurry up and get your coat and boots on. The workmen are waiting to start. This will be so wonderful for us all. I have seen similar contraptions in all the best houses in England," she added.

"Really, Mother! What houses?" I was surprised to hear that, as she never talked about her past.

"Well, I knew Lady Sinclair at Enderby House in London, and she had all the very latest conveniences like this."

I did not press her any further, because the subject was not really of much interest to me, so I just obeyed and got ready to play outside with my obnoxious little brothers.

* * *

We often had picnics on the lawns at Providence, and those were times when Uncle Edward and Uncle James and Aunt Eliza visited us. I would play happily with little Anna and later with Uncle James's other children, Joe and Kit, once they arrived. I even tolerated my twin brothers, Bertie and Teddy, on those occasions.

But I admit that the twins were a terrible bother to me, because they followed me around all the time. This was particularly annoying when I wanted to be alone, like today—or even watching how the workmen put in our new water closets upstairs. But sometimes the twins were also useful, because they would always do my bidding. I referred to them as my little slaves, and Mother was always very annoyed with me about that.

"They are your brothers, Sarah, *not* your slaves. That is very disrespectful," she would say. But I didn't care, because to me they were just little brats.

Nonetheless, I tolerated them on that day because Angelina was there and she always made everything fun whenever we played.

Eventually we were allowed back inside the house, which was now a terrible mess. There was dust everywhere, Mother was bemoaning the fact that it would take the workmen about a week to get everything done. She was pacing up and down in the hall supervising Foo and the maids.

"Can I watch them, mother, when they return tomorrow?"

By then she was so excited by the whole process, I was sure she would have agreed to anything.

"If it will stop your continuous pestering, Sarah, I will allow you to watch," she said. "But be sure to wear your old play clothes tomorrow and not any of your best dresses. And don't get in their way."

"Can we watch too?" echoed my brothers.

"I think not boys. Angelina will keep you both busy in the nursery or outside in the garden."

I smiled smugly and when Mother turned her back, I stuck out my tongue at them. For once I had been favoured and they had not.

* * *

Back in my bedroom, I washed and changed for dinner, anticipating the dreaded seven o'clock gong.

I began to daydream again, thinking this time about the day Sir James Douglas had died. I was told he was a very important man in Victoria. On the day of his funeral, everyone had draped their homes in black cloth and all schools and public places were closed for the day. Although I wasn't quite six years old at the time, his funeral was another occasion when I was allowed to do something with Mother and Papa and the twins weren't. Papa had told me that Sir James helped him when he first arrived in Victoria, and it was important that as his oldest child I should witness this piece of history.

Bishop Cridge had preached a very long, boring sermon and guns rumbled in the distance as we stood by his gravesite in Ross Bay Cemetery. I began to think about death that day and I wondered if guns had rumbled when my other brother Caleb died—but I doubted it. He wasn't as important as Sir James Douglas, except to my mother.

I had also once been a bridesmaid to one of Sir James's daughters, Martha, when she married Mr. Dennis Harris. Mother had seemed delighted that I had been chosen, because the following day the newspaper stated that Miss Martha Douglas's attendants came from Victoria's best families.

Personally, I could not see why that should make her so happy.

*   *   *

One day I woke up to a very quiet house. Foo hadn't made us breakfast or sounded the gong, and I couldn't see Lum working in the garden when I looked out my window.

I met Papa on the stairs as I went downstairs, and he seemed very concerned about something.

"Where is Foo, Papa?" I asked. "Is he sick?"

"No, Sarah, he's not sick. All the Chinese people in Victoria have been told to go on strike today, so he will not be able to work."

"On strike? What does that mean?"

Mother had joined us by then. "Oh, Sarah, stop bothering your father with questions when he has a lot on his mind."

"She is just curious, my dear," said Papa more gently, "so I will explain the situation to her. She should learn about these things."

He then patiently continued. "There is much confusion in the city right now because something called a head tax of fifty dollars a year has been placed on all the Chinese people in Victoria and this is supposed to stop more Chinese from coming. Uncle Edward and I do not agree with this and are trying to do something about it." Well if Papa didn't think it was right, then neither did I.

Uncle Edward was at the front door, and Mother let him in. Then they all went into the library and began discussing the matter.

"The Chinese are far too valuable to our economy," I heard Papa say.

"I agree, Gideon," said Uncle Edward. "I cannot see why they should not be allowed to be here. They have contributed so much to our lives, too."

This whole situation was causing Angelina to have one of her famous "fits". She flitted around and seemed totally anxious all day! When she had one of these "fits" it meant she constantly tapped her large bosom and complained that her heart was fluttering far too fast.

She spent the whole day complaining. "I have the three *anças* to take care of," she screeched in her high-pitched accent to Mother. "I do not cook and clean as well. These little ones—they run me off my feet already."

Much to everyone's relief, Foo and Lum returned to work the next day, after spending the night in Chinatown. Papa explained to me that the Supreme Court had pronounced that the new law was unconstitutional—whatever that meant. I was just relieved that peace reigned once again at Providence, and Mother had resumed playing the piano. It seemed to calm everyone down—especially her.

I don't know why I kept recalling all those memories and thinking about the future. Maybe it was just because my childhood seemed to be going by too fast and I simply wanted to slow it down, hoping it would last forever.

CHAPTER 2

After I turned six, I started school at Craigflower with other children from town.

Every day, we sailed down the Gorge Arm by watercraft. I enjoyed this, because I met other children from all parts of the city, but one day I overheard Mother and Papa discussing my schooling, and it didn't sound good.

Mother wanted me to have a tutor at home, because she thought the school was a bad influence on me. "Sarah is rubbing shoulders with all the riff-raff from town," I heard her say.

"But this will be a good experience for her, to meet other children who are less fortunate than her," Papa replied. "You must agree with that, my dear."

I thanked the good Lord that Papa won that argument, at least for the time being, because I really enjoyed those boating excursions to and from school. The trips were the best part of going to school, and not the hours spent sitting at my school desk. I enjoyed learning, but not sitting still for so long. I always had far too much energy.

My best friend at Craigflower was a native boy called Willow. He was a year older than me and many inches taller, even though I was fairly tall myself, for a girl. He intrigued me because he was unlike all the white children, and even many of the other native boys. His skin was a shade lighter than any of the other native children, and his features were more attractive. The other native children had round, podgy faces, and their skin had an oily texture, but Willow was different. His face was lean, and his skin was clear and firm.

By the time I turned nine, I was madly in love with him and I hung on his every word.

Many people, including my mother, who agreed with her friend, Lady Julia Trutch, thought that all the natives were "savages." I think Mother was afraid of them. Sir Joseph Trutch, Lady Julia's husband and now the Lieutenant Governor of our province, often spoke about them in the most horrid terms. Papa did not agree with their opinions —so neither did I.

Willow was always kind to me, too, whereas many of the other children teased me and called me "stuck up" and "snooty" because I lived in a big house and my parents were rich. One day a girl called Jessica cornered me in the girls' changing room and told me I really had nothing to be proud about.

"After all," she said, "your mother only came here on that old Bride Ship, which means she must have either been an orphan, or a whore looking for a husband, or perhaps both."

Without thinking twice, I swung my hand at her, hit her across the face and made her nose bleed. She screamed at me, and a teacher came running.

Jessica was pointing at me. "She did it. She hit me," she said.

"Sarah, what did you do? I will have to report this disgraceful behavior to your parents," the teacher said, without even waiting for me to explain.

"But she called my mother names," I said, my hand stinging from having hit her so hard.

"That is no excuse, Sarah. I want you to go to the office right now and we will discuss this."

I knew I would be in big trouble, but I didn't care. It felt good to hit Jessie for saying what she did.

On the way home that day, I asked Willow if he knew anything about the Bride Ship. I already knew what a whore was, because I had overheard some of the older children talking about an area of town where some white men visited Chinese ladies for "sexual favors." Those women were called whores, but I had no idea what *sexual favors* were.

Willow seemed to know everything, but his answer about the Bride Ship did not make me feel any better.

"It was called the S.S. *Tynemouth*," he said. "It had a large passenger list, but there were also about sixty women sent out from England by a benevolent society. The women came to work as governesses, or to marry some of the gold miners, because there were not enough white women here then. My parents told me that the ship came in 1862, the same year that smallpox wiped out many of my people."

"Well," I replied, "my mother must just have been an ordinary passenger aboard. I'm sure she came here first class, and she would certainly not have been sent out here as a charity case."

He smiled his gentle smile. "Sarah, it doesn't matter. I am sure your mother is a good woman, so what difference could it make how or why she came to Victoria? She was just one of many colonists."

I knew he was probably right, but my inquisitive mind wanted to know more, so that night I asked Papa. He did not reply immediately, and then he said, rather sternly, "Sarah, is this connected to why I have received this note from your teacher at Craigflower about your bad behavior?" He waved a piece of paper in front of me. "He says you hit another girl. Is that right?"

"Yes, Papa." I never dared lie to Papa.

"But why?"

"Because she insulted Mother. She said Mother came here on that old Bride Ship, just looking for a husband, and that she must have been an orphan, or a—whore, Papa."

"Sarah, I never want to hear you use that word again. It is despicable. One day, I am sure your mother will tell you herself about her life before she came to Victoria, but never, ever listen to such odious gossip. Your mother worked as a governess for a while here before we were married, but she was, and is, a good woman. Never forget that. We will not speak of this again, do you hear?"

"Yes, Papa." I had never seen him that angry.

"And you will apologize to the girl you hit. Even her insult to your mother does not give you the right to hit her. That is most unladylike."

"Yes, Papa."

"You have much of your mother's spirit in you," he said. "But you must try and curb your temper, even when—well, even when you know you might be right." He looked at me long and hard and then said, "And now you may go, lassie."

I loved it when he called me *lassie* because it reminded me of the stories he told us about Scotland, where he was born.

I was then dismissed from his study, but I sensed a smile would appear on his face before I turned my back. I was sure, deep down, he was proud of the way I had dealt with Jessie at school.

I know I was—and I didn't regret that I had hit her at all.

* * *

Willow frequently got off at my stop from the school boat, even though he lived farther away, on the other side of town. He said he preferred to walk the rest of the way, but this gave us time to talk privately together behind our boathouse. He told me stories of his ancestors who had lived on the Songhees land. Many of his people, including his grandfather, had fled Victoria in 1862 because of the smallpox epidemic, or scourge, as he called it, but his father and mother later returned with their children because the winters were milder here. They now lived on the reserve.

"That was our land once, Sarah," he said. "And the Legwunten people lived for many generations on the land your house is built on."

"I didn't know that, Willow. But my father purchased this land from the government."

"Ah yes ... the government! The almighty Hudson Bay Company." He sounded angry for a moment. "But I intend to become educated," he told me in his almost perfect English. He refused to speak to me in the Chinook language in which many of the other native children communicated, although he did teach me some of their words.

"One day I will be someone important and will not be called Willow Running Bear. I will take the name William Baron. What do you think of that, Miss Sarah?"

"I think it sounds very grand, Willow. But you should not be ashamed of being Songhees, either."

"Ah, a wise girl." He grinned. "You have remembered what I taught you. But no, I will never forget my roots, and I will fight for the rights and freedoms of my people. Perhaps I will become a lawyer like your uncles, the Caldwells."

"Perhaps." I sighed. At that point I believed everything he told me. After all, he was so tall and handsome, and he was my first love, so I was sure he could do just about anything to which he put his mind.

But during the summer of my eleventh year, two things happened that brought my relationship with Willow to an unhappy conclusion.

CHAPTER 3

The first happened on the Saturday we had planned an excursion to Dead Man's Island.

We often passed that small island on our way to school, and Willow told me that one day he would bring his canoe and take me there. I was a little afraid, because I had heard it was the burial ground for native people and there had been rumours of ghostly sightings there. However, the day we chose for our adventure was bright and sunny, and I easily slipped away from Angelina and Foo's protective eyes early in the morning, telling them I was taking my easel down to the water to paint.

I did not particularly enjoy painting or doing any of the other ladylike things young girls were supposed to do, like playing the piano or embroidery, so Foo raised his eyebrows slightly, but he seemed to believe my story. Angelina promised to keep Bertie and Teddy occupied so they would not bother me.

Willow was waiting for me by the boathouse, and I eagerly climbed into his canoe, leaving my easel and paints propped up against a tree, so that if anyone came looking for me they would know I had been there and had probably just wandered off for a few moments.

Willow was barefoot and as he rowed us off in the boat, I became intrigued by his brown feet. They were lean and handsome and made me feel terribly overdressed in my laced-up boots. It only took a few minutes to reach the island and for Willow to maneuver the craft to the opposite side of it.

"There is a small lagoon on this side of the island, Sarah, and we can swim there," he said.

"Swim? But I don't have a bathing costume," I replied.

"No matter—you will soon see."

It was the most idyllic place, well-hidden and surrounded by tall trees and shrubbery. It was quite private and even had a sandy surround, like the beach alongside the ocean. Willow had brought a blanket, which he spread out on the sand. He then proceeded to strip off his clothing until, much to my embarrassment, he stood before me completely naked except for a very small loin cloth covering his most private parts. He took my hand and led me to the water's edge, both of us leaving footprints in the wet sand.

"Come, Sarah, it is much better to swim with no clothes on."

"Oh, Willow, I think not. My mother would not approve."

"Can she see you now?"

"No."

"Well then?"

Before I realized it, I was removing my heavy boots and had pulled down my stockings. The sand felt wonderful on my now bare feet. I slowly lifted my cumbersome dress over my head and stood in my camisole and bloomers, feeling very daring.

And then Willow removed his loin cloth and I turned my head away as he dived into the pool, calling to me.

"Come, Sarah, *all* your clothing. The water is warm and very soothing to the bare skin."

In one quick move, I dispensed with the rest of my clothing and dived into the pool beside Willow. Despite my feelings for him, these actions seemed completely innocent at the time as we splashed around in the water in an abandoned, unrestrained way. Our bodies frequently touched, but it was nothing more than childish play.

After a while, we emerged from the water and ran across the sand to our blanket. On the way, I hastily grabbed my clothes left at the water's edge and began to dress.

"Let the sun dry our bodies first, Sarah," said Willow. It certainly made sense, but nonetheless I decided to cover the most private areas of my body with my camisole while we waited for the sun to dry us.

"Look, Sarah," whispered Willow. "Look back at the sand. See how our footprints are side by side, heading down to the water, and they look so different."

"Yes, mine are smaller than yours."

"Not just that. Mine are free, but yours were enclosed in boots. But see on this side, as we ran back up the sand, our footprints are the same. We're both free."

I nodded. He was right, and it felt good to be free and unencumbered. When the sun momentarily slipped behind a cloud, I began to feel a chill and so hastily began to dress again. I did not put my stockings or shoes back on, though.

I was rather relieved to see Willow dressing too, because his lean, brown body was now becoming a bewildering distraction, and I began to feel stirrings deep in the pit of my stomach that I did not fully understand.

We nibbled on some bread that Willow had brought, and we talked of many things. The time slipped by so quickly, and I realized we had been gone a long while and someone was sure to be looking for me by now.

"We must go now, Willow. I don't want to, but I'm sure I'll be in trouble if I stay away much longer."

He took my hand as we stood up. "I'll get you safely back, my Sarah," he said gently. "Do not fear."

He rowed quickly back down the Arm towards our boathouse, but I knew before we reached the landing that I was most definitely in *big* trouble. Both Papa and Mother were standing on the launching ramp, with Angelina and Foo behind them, and my two annoying little brothers were full of glee as they jumped around.

Bertie was chanting, "Sarah's in trouble! Sarah's in trouble!" And Teddy was giggling. Angelina, of course, was clasping her hands to her breast while intermittently genuflecting and praising God for my safe return. Papa was looking particularly stern. Mother simply looked mortified.

*   *   *

Willow rowed into land and helped me out of the canoe.

"And just *where* do you think you have been, Sarah?" Mother said in her most angry voice.

"My apologies, Mrs. McBride. I took Sarah to show her our people's island burial place. We lost track of the time—but she was quite safe with me."

Mother snorted her disapproval and glanced down at my bare feet covered in sand.

Papa said, "You have had us all worried, Willow. Sarah was told only that she could come down to the water to paint. She didn't ask for permission to leave the grounds, and naturally we were all very worried."

"Yes, sir," said Willow. "I am indeed very sorry for the distress we've caused you."

"Distress!" Mother raised her voice to a high pitch. "Distress!" she repeated. "Can you imagine how worried we were? No, I am sure you cannot! So, take your boat and leave, young man. My daughter does not mix with people like you."

Willow looked hurt, and I was horrified. I knew Papa was angered by her remark, because he glared at my mother.

"Off you go now, Willow," he said, somewhat more gently. "My wife is naturally upset, as she was so worried about our daughter."

And with that, Willow left and we all climbed the steps leading back to Providence. As we walked along, Mother continued berating me, telling me how unseemly my behavior was.

"You have come home half-dressed and barefoot, with sand all over you. What could you have been doing? And with whom? An *Indian* no less?" she said.

I failed to understand her concern. What difference could it make that Willow was Songhees? Many of his people worked with Papa, and he respected them. And we employed Chinese people, such as Ah Foo and Lum, whom we all adored. And besides, Skiff, one of Papa's closest friends and work colleagues, who also worked in the garden at Providence, and his wife, Dulcie, who was Mama's companion, were both black. I pointed all this out to my parents as we returned to the house, but neither seemed inclined to discuss it.

Teddy and Bertie continued to giggle and chant their silly little refrains about how bad I had been, until finally even Papa became irritated and told them to head to their rooms immediately. I was sent to my room too and told to stay there for the remainder of the day. That evening Mother came and told me, quite bluntly, that I would not be allowed to associate with Willow ever again, and instead I must find friends of my own kind.

"But Willow *is* my friend," I screamed.

"That's enough, Sarah. We will not discuss this anymore."

"I hate you! I hate you!"

She turned and left my room, closing the door behind her.

I cried myself to sleep after telling my mother that I would hate her forever. But, forever is a very long while, and of course we could not keep up a continual battle between us. Eventually we formed a cold truce, but she still forbade me to see Willow.

"Your activities will be monitored during school hours also, Sarah," she said the next morning. "So, I do not want to hear that you are associating with that native boy there, either."

A few days later, while I was lying in my favorite place on the staircase, I overheard her discussing the possibility of hiring a tutor for us all.

"I have heard of this splendid man, Gideon. His name is Hugh Davenport, and he comes from England and is an excellent teacher," she told Papa in the library. "Please say we can hire him for Sarah and the boys? I think it is far more appropriate than having them attend Craigflower, now that they are all getting older."

"Em—I'll think about it, my dear. But sometimes I just don't understand why you are so against other races. It makes no sense. Dulcie and Skiff are our best friends."

"That's different. They are not *Indians*."

Oh, how that grated on my ears!

"And you have always insisted that I should become a lady in my position as your wife. Well, ladies don't behave the way Sarah is behaving. I want to make sure *she* has all the benefits that I never had—even though I should have."

I heard Papa sigh as Mother continued her pleading.

"Oh Gideon, please do more than just think about it. I really believe that Sarah needs to go away to boarding school, but you won't hear of that yet, so this is a wonderful compromise. And she will no longer be mixing with the wrong people. I have always tried so hard to achieve that for our family, ever since you told me we are now a part of the elite."

"My dear woman, I never believed she *was* mixing with the wrong people, but if you think a tutor would help with her education, we'll give this fellow a try."

A tutor! How ghastly, I thought. That would mean I would be confined to the house all day and not able to mix with anyone. Actually, there was only one person I wanted to see, and that was Willow. I missed him terribly.

The following week, an envelope arrived, addressed to me. Foo handed it to me, saying that a young boy had given it to Lum down by the boathouse. Foo seemed to understand who it had come from and appeared nervous when he gave it to me. I knew immediately who had sent it. Inside was a short poem called "Footprints." I read it quickly.

Two footprints in the sand,

One broad and heavy,
One lean and nimble
One encased in the boot of civilization,
One bare and browned by the sun.
One walking, tamed by leather.
One running, wild in freedom.
One trodden down in authority,
One white,
One brown.
Such are our footprints in the sand.
It was signed
With love from William Baron.

I cried myself to sleep again that night, thinking of my first love and feeling how tragic it was to be parted simply because of our stations in life.

The following morning, I awoke to discover the second great happening of my eleventh summer. My monthly courses had arrived, and, according to Mother, I was now "a woman." This seemed particularly senseless to me. I was being treated like a child when it came to who I should or should not associate with, but would now be considered "a woman" simply because of some biological event taking place inside my body—an event, I might add, that was both annoying and unpleasant.

The arrival of this "event" would, I felt sure, make my Mother even more determined to keep me isolated from all unwanted male attention, no matter who the male might be. It had probably merely confirmed her decision to prevent me from seeing Willow ever again.

What a preposterous and totally unreasonable world it was!

CHAPTER 4

As it happened, Mr. Davenport turned out to be perfect. He was quiet, unassuming and certainly not very strict. Best of all, I could twist him around my little finger with very little effort.

My two brothers were the perfect students and sat obediently at their desks doing the work assigned to them, with very little prompting. Mr. Davenport was always delighted with their progress. I was a different matter and proved much more difficult.

"I'm bored with the assignments Mr. Davenport gives us," I told my parents one day. "And I hate sitting at a desk for so long."

Poor Mr. Davenport tried his very best to keep me occupied and interested, but he knew from the very beginning that he was fighting a losing battle. However, being of an easygoing nature, he preferred not to fight with me or reprimand me if I failed to complete the work he had assigned us. It was easier for him to allow me to get away with being idle, or simply to permit me to leave the classroom and escape to the garden, rather than argue the point with me. I frequently told him I had a headache or I simply needed fresh air, and he seemed only too happy to see me leave.

One day, I overheard my parents discussing the situation. "Gideon, what are we to do with her?" Mother said.

"Don't worry, my dear. I'm sure she will eventually find her own way in the world."

"But, Gideon, one day I caught her leaving the house and heading for the stables, and before I had time to stop her, she had saddled up her horse and taken off. The situation simply cannot continue. Mr. Davenport can't seem to control her, and she has far too much freedom away from her books."

So, by the end of the summer of 1882, my parents made another decision concerning my future education.

*   *   *

"But, Mother, *why* do I have to go away to school?" I asked for the millionth time.

"Sarah, do stop being so unreasonable. Going to Angela College is not really going away. You will simply be a weekly boarder and will return every weekend to Providence."

"But it's a girls' school and so straitlaced, and it is way over on the other side of town," I argued.

Papa laughed at that. "Dear child, it is no distance away. Just up on Burdett Hill, near the cathedral, and it comes highly recommended."

"Oh Papa, you don't want me to go away every week, do you?"

Mother immediately stepped in. "Now, young lady, stop that immediately. Your father and I are both in agreement that this is the best compromise. You will be twelve years old at the end of this year, so starting at Angela College in September will be perfect. Besides, it will prepare you for any future education back east—or even in Europe."

"Europe!" I screeched. "Oh God!"

"It will also improve your manner of speaking," she said, looking at me in disapproval at my blasphemy. "They might even manage to make a lady out of you."

"I don't want to be a lady! I want to be me, and I want to stay at Providence forever."

"Now, now, sweetpea," said Papa gently. I loved it when he called me by his pet name. "You will be here every weekend and we can still ride together, or I can take you sailing, but during the week you will board at the school and make some wonderful new friends."

"I doubt it, Papa. They will all be the daughters of Mother's stuck-up friends, I suppose."

Papa laughed out loud, and Mother glared at him. "Gideon, don't encourage her, please. Sarah, it is all arranged. We have an interview with the headmistress, Miss Garthwaite, next week, and you will be starting there at the beginning of September."

"What about Bertie and Teddy? Why are they allowed to stay at home?"

"They will be tutored by Mr. Davenport for at least another year, and then most likely will enter Upper Canada College in Toronto, where your Uncle James attended, so they will have to travel much farther away."

"Well, they're boys, and they're little brats anyway. They deserve to go away."

Papa was still laughing, and I was becoming more and more irritated by them both. Finally I was dismissed and told to go to my room until dinner was ready. Instead, I lingered upstairs on the landing, listening to their continuing conversation.

"Gideon, you don't help matters at all by laughing. Please read the prospectus for Angela College again. It sounds perfect for Sarah. And it was named Angela College in recognition of its benefactress, Angela Burdett-Coutts. She was the same lady who sponsored the *Tynemouth.* I even saw her at Enderby House on occasion."

"I know you are impressed with the school, my dear," replied Papa, and then I heard him begin to read out loud.

"For those parents who cannot bear to part with their beloved daughters at such a tender age by sending them back to England for any length of time, Angela College is the perfect answer. The College offers all that is best in a rounded English education right here in Victoria in a delightful, healthy, high area of the city, close to the Cathedral Church and opposite the residence of the Bishop." He turned the page.

"I guess it does sound like what we feel she needs," he commented. "And rates are very reasonable at only $30 every month for Sarah as a weekly boarder. According to this, subjects taught include French,

German, drawing, botany, astronomy, religious instruction, arithmetic and English, in addition to piano, art and drama. My goodness!"

He continued to read from the prospectus.

"*Our prime objective is to give the young girls of Victoria a sound religious, moral and secular education, and to place within the reach of the greatest possible number, in this our distant home, the means of forming the habits of character of an English lady as we mold them into refined and gracious young women.*"

Papa then began to laugh, and I found myself smiling also because I knew we were both thinking the same thing. No one, however hard they might try, would *ever* mold me into anything that I didn't want to be.

CHAPTER 5

Angela College was a red-brick, Gothic revival structure set high up on Cathedral Hill, looking down its elegant Anglican nose towards Humboldt Street and the spacious grounds of St. Ann's Academy, which provided a Catholic education for the lower classes.

The Angela, with its spire pointing skyward to glory, fancied itself as something rather special, providing an all-round Anglican education for the middle- and upper-class girls of Victoria.

One morning in early September, we drove up the hill in our carriage towards the school. I was wearing my respectable navy-blue dress trimmed with a white lace collar. I hated it. We alighted under the porte cochere and were escorted through the entrance hall to the headmistress's office, down a long corridor with walls lined in dark mahogany.

Miss Garthwaite was an austere-looking woman with tiny *pince nez* spectacles on the end of her long nose. She greeted us like old friends and invited my parents to sit in the two armchairs opposite her desk. I was expected to remain standing as she looked me up and down.

"I am delighted to meet you both again, Captain and Mrs. McBride."

"And Sarah." She put on a watery smile as she spoke directly to me. "I am sure you will be very happy with us."

"Sarah is looking forward to starting school, Miss Garthwaite," Mother said. "Her education so far, as we explained at our previous meeting, has been confined to Craigflower School and a private tutor, but she is a bright girl and very willing to learn."

"As are all our girls," replied Miss Garthwaite. "They must *all* be willing to learn. It is a prerequisite."

"Of course."

"We wish Sarah to board from Mondays to Fridays," interjected Papa. "Every Friday after school she will be met by our carriage driver and brought home, returning to school on Sunday nights."

"Of course," said Miss Garthwaite. "Now, while we discuss fees and so on, I will ask Miss Brady, my assistant, to escort Sarah to the room she will be sharing with another girl. She will also be shown the uniform she will wear during the week."

A uniform! I shuddered,

"With whom will Sarah be sharing a room?" Mother asked. "I hope it will be someone suitable."

"Yes. indeed—a charming young girl who is also starting with us this week. Her name is Margaret Bowers, the daughter of Sir William and Lady Bowers. Sir William is with the Dominion foreign service and has been posted to London for two years, so Margaret will be boarding with us full-time."

Mother looked delighted, but Margaret Bowers sounded too respectable for my liking.

Miss Brady entered the room at that point. I assumed she had been summoned by an invisible bell beneath Miss Garthwaite's desk.

"Say your farewells to your parents now, Sarah, and then off you go. You will soon settle in, I'm sure."

I hugged Papa tightly and then kissed Mother dutifully on the cheek. I had never felt so utterly miserable in my life.

* * *

I was determined not to cry or show any emotion, but I felt like I was entering a prison. My childhood was over, and now I was entering a place of confinement where I would be deprived of my freedom. But then, I always did have a sense of the dramatic!

Miss Brady was a chirpy little person who tried to joke as she tripped along the corridor ahead of me and then up the massive staircase to the dormitories above.

"You're in Room 333," she said. "It's an easy number to remember, Sarah." *More like Cell 333,* I thought, as we entered the room.

It was minuscule compared to my bedroom at Providence. It barely had space for two narrow beds, two dressers and two small desks. My uniform was laid out on one bed, along with my small valise, which had already been sent up. On the other bed sat a girl who looked almost as stunned and horrified as I felt.

"Sarah McBride, Margaret Bowers," said Miss Brady. "Shake hands, girls. You have one hour to unpack and change into your uniforms, and when the bell rings you are to come down to the auditorium, where your weekly schedules will be handed out, with your lesson plans. Don't be late." And with that she was gone.

Margaret Bowers and I stared at one another as though we had been placed on another planet. And then we both laughed at the same time.

"Hello," she said. "I'll call you Bridey, for McBride."

I nodded. "Fine with me. I'll call you Bowery, then. For Bowers."

So Bridey and Bowery we were, from that day forth. As we chatted, we got to know each other.

"I was born in February 1872," she began.

"Then I'm two months older than you. My birthday's in December 1871."

"You're much taller than me," said Bowery. "And my hair is so mousey-brown and straight, but yours is such a beautiful auburn-red color—and so curly." She sighed.

"I envy you your well-behaved hair. Mine is always a mess."

We decided that life was definitely unfair because we were always given the opposite of what we wanted.

Despite our initial misgivings about Angela College, Bowery and I became best friends that day, and she made life there bearable for me. But within a few days I realized she was an excellent student, whereas I was a complete dunce.

That is, until I met Miss Howard, the drama teacher, during the second week of my servitude. It was then that I discovered what I was really good at in life and, more importantly, what I really enjoyed. Acting!

Had I chosen watercolor painting, embroidery, French or music, I might well have gained some praise and approval from my mother, but *acting*! In her opinion, only women of the lower classes or worse made a living on the stage.

"It is all well and good to 'play-act' in drama productions at school, especially if it happens to be Shakespeare, which will always be well received, but to talk about one day going to London, New York or Paris and making your living as an actress on the stage is completely unacceptable, Sarah!" she told me when I first mentioned it.

Of course I had said those things just to irritate her. I really had no desire to become a great world-famous actress. I simply wanted to live at Providence and ride my horse, but I did enjoy the feeling whenever I was on stage and expressing myself in a dramatic fashion. It was a world of make-believe where I could be someone completely different. A wonderful escape from everyday life. And I knew I was good at it. Miss Howard praised me constantly, and this, of course, boosted my confidence and convinced me of my acting abilities.

So, every weekend when I went home, I continued to irritate my mother by talking of dreams of one day becoming an actress

CHAPTER 6

I was soon allowed to invite Bowery to stay for weekends at Providence, and those times were especially fun.

Papa often rode with us out to Cadboro Bay, and at other times, family picnics were arranged on the lawn at Providence, where the whole family, including the Caldwells, joined in. Anna and Joe Caldwell and their new little brother Christopher (called Kit), and we three McBride children and Bowery, always made it a noisy and fun-filled occasion.

Angelina now had less and less to do, because her *crianças* were all grown up, and it hardly seemed likely that Mother and Papa would produce more children. However she continued to complain of being overworked.

I hoped that, as our nanny, she would stay on forever as our companion or, at worst, be allowed to remain as a family retainer. I was sure Papa would never discard her or send her away. Mary, Foo, Lum, Skiff and Dulcie were also a part of our family, and I could not imagine Providence without any of them.

Bowery loved staying with us, and she soon wrote to her parents asking if she could spend every weekend at Providence and become a weekly boarder, like me. My parents both approved of this arrangement and extended their invitation to the Bowers family in London. They liked Bowery and felt she would be a good influence on me, because she was smart and much more ladylike than I was. If only they knew the mischief we got up to together, mostly at my instigation.

Teddy developed an enormous crush on Bowery, even though she was more than a year older. Bowery thought it was terribly amusing. She treated him with disdain at first but still allowed him to follow her around like a love-sick puppy and do her bidding. Bertie, who hadn't yet discovered an interest in girls, thought his brother was being totally ridiculous.

I celebrated my twelfth birthday during the Christmas holidays from school that year and, much to my delight, Bowery was allowed to stay with us because her parents did not return to Canada for Christmas. The house was decorated with laurel and other greenery, and we installed an enormous fir tree in the hall that all the children helped decorate, with Foo being in charge.

Mother had even been pleased with me because she said my art work had improved, as well as my singing, and she allowed me to accompany her at the piano. Once I started talking about drama again, though, an expression crossed her face that I read only too well. It said: *Sarah is being troublesome—again!*

That Christmas day, the house was full of McBrides and Caldwells. Uncle Edward walked over from James Bay through the snow, laden down with an abundance of gifts. Soon after, a carriage arrived with Uncle James, Aunt Eliza, Anna, Joe and little Kit, now Christopher's established nickname. We greeted everyone at the door with hugs and laughter, and soon the house was full of noise and hilarity.

Bowery and I shared my bedroom over the holiday, and it was the most marvelous Christmas ever. By then, I had also confided in Bowery about my great love for Willow, but I was able to discuss it now in a more adult way. I believed I had almost recovered from my passion.

"There will be many other passions in the years to come, Sarah. You are made for great love affairs." Then we giggled mercilessly.

We all ate far too much, and later we sang carols around the tree and played charades. The men then retired to Papa's library to smoke and drink port and the ladies to the drawing room. We children were allowed to stay up really late, playing games in the nursery.

When the guests had all left and my little brothers were in bed, I showed Bowery my secret place on the staircase. She thought it was great fun to eavesdrop on my parents, who were still talking down below in Papa's library.

We giggled as they discussed the happenings of the evening and the antics of Uncle James while we played charades. Papa then said something terribly romantic to Mother about how beautiful she looked. He held her in his arms and they kissed as they swayed together.

"Oh God," I whispered. "Now they're going to be all romantic again."

Bowery looked at me rather sadly for a moment. "How lucky you are to have parents who love each other," she said. And with that, she stood up and tiptoed back to my bedroom, leaving me to ponder her words and think about something I had never considered before. Love between a husband and a wife.

A rare commodity. I wondered, would it ever be mine?

*　*　*

Before we returned to school in January, Papa had a telephone machine installed in the hall at Providence. This newfangled creation was the bane of Foo's life, for it made him jump about three feet in the air every time it rang, and Angelina was so petrified of it that she simply refused to have anything to do with it. It was amusing to watch their reactions, but Mother told me she felt very comforted by it because now she would have contact with our school immediately in the event of an emergency.

Bowery and I returned to school with new energy and spirit. She had been very impressed by her stay at Providence and Mother's constant reminiscing about Princess Louise's visit to our house in October, when she dined there with her husband, the governor-general of Canada.

"Imagine," said Bowery, putting on her best airs-and-graces voice, "I actually sat at the same table as the Queen's daughter, my dear—maybe even on the same chair!"

"Oh, and was it still warm?" I giggled.

"Oh, definitely, my dear. It still bore the royal imprint!"

"God, my mother is *such* a snob!" I replied. "I was so embarrassed to have her go on and on about the royal visit and how much the princess absolutely adored Providence and didn't want to leave—blah blah blah."

"Oh, Bridey, your mother is really a poppet. She can't help being proud of her beautiful home."

"Em—maybe, but what's *so* special about a princess? And why does my mother have to keep boasting about everything?"

But eventually I learned to accept my mother for who she was, and she, in turn, accepted me the way I was. The routine of life at Angela College during the week and then weekends at Providence continued over the next two years, and with the help of Miss Howard and my natural talent for drama, I somehow managed to survive it all.

*   *   *

Papa was more involved in business trips during this period, so was not always home at weekends. He and Uncle Edward were also deeply involved in finding ways to improve our city, so I felt proud of them both.

One weekend when he was home, Papa told us an amusing story about city hall which had us all hooting with laughter.

"It all began with a judgment being made against the City," he told us. "It was for a paltry sum of $707 plus change and was brought by Drake & Johnson, but dear Mr. Carey, our stuffy mayor, refused to pay it. So, the high sheriff was called to City Hall in great splendour to seize all the city's books, assessment rolls, and spare cash. Can you imagine it?"

We all shook our heads in horror.

"Then a seal was placed on the safe and the bailiff was positioned outside the building on guard. And then, if you please, the sheriff announced he would hold a public auction of the unopened safe and all of the City's furniture, rock-crushers, horses, and even the dump carts."

"Whatever happened next, Papa?" I asked.

"Well, a number of citizens, including myself and your Great Uncle Edward, each offered to pay $75 towards that silly disputed bill so that the matter could be settled once and for all. Thank goodness the offer was accepted and the auction did not go ahead, but Mr. Carey still threatened to sue the sheriff, if you please, for $25,000."

"Good heavens!"

"He also refused to take back the furniture which had been seized. It was so childish, but quite amusing to the onlookers."

Mother spoke at this point. "Hardly any wonder that Mr. Carey has not been re-elected as mayor for the coming term. Our dear friend, Bob Rithet, will make an excellent mayor. You know, your father was even urged to run, but he declined."

"Oh Papa, were you really?"

"Yes, and I decided not to get myself involved. The business of politics is too conniving and under-handed for me."

"And you, my dear, are far too honest a man." Mother smiled.

"But Uncle Edward is a politician, and he is honest."

"Edward is a rare exception," said Papa.

* * *

And then, in 1886, the long-awaited transcontinental railway drew nearer to reality. The last spike for that railway had been driven at a place called Craigellachie the previous November.

Papa frequently met with Mr. William Van Horne, who was staying at the Driard Hotel, the grandest establishment in town. They discussed where the railway terminus would be on the mainland. They also talked of a planned steamship service from Burrard Inlet to both Nanaimo and Victoria, which of course was of particular interest to Papa because of his transport businesses.

During our school summer holiday that year, the first train from eastern Canada reached Port Moody, but the definite highlight of the month for Mother was a visit by the Prime Minister himself, Sir John A. Macdonald. She became less enamoured of him, however, when Papa told her about his views on Indigenous people. The new rules he was bringing in for the people he considered "savages" were not acceptable to men like my father.

Nonetheless, the McBrides entertained the Macdonalds for dinner one night at Providence. Dear Foo ran around in a panic all day as he prepared the menu with the help of Dulcie. I personally was glad that Sir John and Lady Macdonald were staying at the Driard Hotel and not with us.

And then in August, during our school holidays, we were all invited to a most historic ceremony at Cliffside, near Shawnagan Lake, when Sir John himself pounded home a golden spike with a silver sledgehammer to mark the completion of the Esquimalt and Nanaimo Railway.

Bowery's parents did not return to Canada for the Christmas of 1886, so once again she was invited to spend the holidays with us and help celebrate my fifteenth birthday.

My parents had decided that the following summer I would attend a finishing school in Europe, and I begged them to contact Bowery's parents in London to see if they could arrange for her to go to the same school. It was in a place called Dresden in Saxony, and I would be there for two years at least.

When a letter came from Bowery's parents agreeing that it would be a wonderful idea because they would be nearer their "beloved daughter," Bowery and I danced around my bedroom in joy. I was thrilled she and I would not be separated, but I hardly thought of her as her parents' "beloved daughter" when they had taken practically no interest in her welfare, or even visited her, since they first left for London almost four years earlier.

My two infuriating brothers would finally be leaving for Upper Canada College in Toronto at the same time, and we would all travel across Canada by train to deposit them there, before continuing on to New York to catch a liner across the Atlantic Ocean to England.

Because of these events, Papa had decided that Angelina should be allowed to retire, but he intended to take care of her as a family retainer in her retirement. He had a small cottage built near the entrance gates to Providence which would become Angelina's retirement home.

She was delighted, and Mother insisted on calling the cottage "The Lodge," which made it sound much grander than it really was.

* * *

Our departure was still a few months away, so Bowery and I continued to live one day at a time. We decided to celebrate the fact that we would be heading to Europe together by smoking cigars! I found two in Papa's smoking room, and the next weekend, we headed down to the boathouse to try them out.

We puffed and blew and finally inhaled until we both felt violently sick and simultaneously lost our lunches in a heap on the ground. We then hurriedly attempted to cover up the evidence of our recklessness with grass from the compost pile, but I am sure that Foo suspected what we had been up to. As usual, however, he was loyal and did not repeat his suspicions to my parents.

Of course, Teddy still adored Bowery and vowed that their separation to different parts of the world would be but nothing in the overall scheme of things. He wrote her a long, impassioned letter, stating that once he had become an established doctor, which at that time seemed to be his one goal in life, he would propose marriage to her. Bowery read me the letter and then clutched it dramatically to her breast.

"Teddy is *so* sweet, Bridey. I could easily grow to love him eventually—and just think, we would be sisters-in-law."

"*That,* my dear Bowery, is the only good thing about it. My little brother is an absolute pain. Even Bertie would be a better choice for you. He is more like Papa and will, I am sure, one day be a businessman of note."

"But Teddy is so much more sensitive!"

"Sensitive! Bah," I said. "He's a complete fool."

An episode a week later convinced Bowery that I might be right.

CHAPTER 7

Teddy's passion in life was medicine. He wanted to save the world, he said, and his particular field of interest was medical research.

He followed Dr. Ralph around whenever he was allowed to do so, constantly bombarding the poor man with a million questions. How does this work? What is this about? What does this symptom mean? And he was extremely interested in all the latest research and read every medical book he could lay his hands on.

Hardly surprising, therefore, that one day he would eventually find a willing patient to experiment on. The poor unfortunate patient happened to be Cain, one of our faithful old mongrel dogs.

Cain, in his advancing years, appeared to be suffering from a problem on his right front paw, and Mother had said she would call the animal doctor to take a look at it because Cain was limping badly. Meanwhile, however, Teddy decided to take the matter into his own hands, having discussed the latest forms of anesthesia with Dr. Ralph, who had no idea that his young, adoring student intended to put those discussions into practice.

On one particularly hot, sunny Saturday afternoon in May, Bowery and I headed down to the Arm with our parasols and some books, having no idea that something ominous was taking place behind the garden shed. We spread out a blanket by the water and blissfully watched the activity on the Arm for a while. It was pleasant passing the time with no interruptions from my brothers, but eventually the sun felt too hot, so we headed back up the lawn.

Spotting the twins, Bowery said she wanted to talk to Teddy, so we wandered over to them. Cain lay on the ground, appearing to be asleep. The boys were deep in discussion.

"What's wrong with Cain?" I asked.

"He's sleeping," replied Teddy.

I bent over him, with Bowery beside me. We both shook Cain gently but he did not stir. "Oh my goodness," said Bowery, almost in tears. "I think he may be dead."

"He's *not* dead," announced Teddy, with all the certainty of a dedicated physician. "He's simply anaesthetized. And his paw is bandaged because I operated on it."

"You did *what?*" I screamed at him.

"I operated on his dewclaw, which is no longer in-grown and is fine now."

"You stupid little idiot," I screamed. "His paw might be fine, but he won't wake up, so something must be wrong."

"Calm down, sister dear," said Teddy. "I just misjudged the amount of the anesthetic. Next time I'll get it right. He's sleeping a little longer than necessary."

"Next time! Next time! There will be *no* next time, Edward Gideon McBride! Quick, Bowery, help me get a bucket of water. We'll throw it over him and maybe that will revive him. We can't possibly leave him like this."

Teddy had apparently procured some mysterious concoction from Dr. Ralph's office that was used to anaesthetize patients in preparation for minor surgical procedures. Unfortunately, he had not correctly assessed the amount to be used for a body of Cain's age and weight. In addition to this discrepancy, he had no information as to whether it would even work on an animal!

Nonetheless, with the assistance of his equally inept twin, he had dosed Cain with what he thought was a small portion of the magic liquid, and once it had sent poor Cain into dreamland, proceeded to cut away the offending claw. The operation was a success in itself, but rousing poor Cain was not so easy.

And so the four of us ran for water and threw it over Cain, who eventually opened his eyes, stood up and shook himself, a dazed expression on his face. He did, however, walk a few steps without a limp, and within a week, his paw had healed and he was running around the grounds like his old self again.

But it took a long time for me to forgive my brother for his stupidity, and even Bowery suggested to him that he should refrain from experimenting on anyone, including animals, until he was at least a qualified medical student.

Teddy, of course, listened to Bowery's pleas far more than he did to my reprimands.

* * *

In early June of 1887, we all set off on what my mother described as our educational adventure.

Accompanied by Mother and Papa, Bowery and I, who were both still a few months short of sixteen, and Teddy and Bertie, who would be fifteen in October, departed from New Westminster together on one of the earliest trains to cross the continent. We had previously heard the Prime Minister's wife, Lady Macdonald, praise this incredible form of travel and the magnificent scenery along the way, but we were utterly unprepared for just how beautiful the journey would actually be.

I think it left us all in awe of the immense size and distinction of our country. Even Papa, who had travelled through Rupert's Land with the Hudson's Bay Company in his youth, and later through much of California, Oregon and British Columbia on business, declared he had not seen country to compare with the mountainous splendour of the Rocky Mountain range. We all agreed that the railway was an incredible engineering feat as it tunnelled and bridged its way through unimaginably difficult terrain.

Later we passed through the flatlands of Prairie country, and then journeyed on towards Ontario, by which time we were experiencing greener country dotted with lakes. Finally we reached Toronto itself, and a carriage took us from the railway station to Upper Canada College on Russell Square.

As we drove towards the imposing edifice, Papa gave us a history lesson on the school from which Uncle James had graduated before going on to study law at McGill to become a lawyer with his father's firm.

"It's the oldest independent school in the Province of Ontario," he told us, "and was founded in 1829 by the then Lieutenant-Governor of the British Colony of Upper Canada. The school has a very auspicious history as a non-denominational school for boys."

"It is highly thought of, even in England," added Mother with pride as her gloved hand patted each of her sons, in a gesture that looked as if she were anointing them into greatness. Bowery and I looked at each other and giggled.

"There is a rumour that the school will move to a larger site within the next few years," said Papa. "Expansion is badly needed, with such a great increase in student population."

We all nodded solemnly. "The school is simply *too* prestigious for words," I offered. Mother glared at my sarcasm, even though I'd meant it to be a joke.

Bowery and I were told to stay in the carriage while Mother and Papa took the twins inside. An hour passed before they emerged, the boys to say their farewells to us. They both seemed very excited about the school and their accommodations, but Teddy of course looked devastated at saying goodbye to Bowery.

"I will write to you faithfully," I heard him promise her. I doubted that he would write to me, his irritating sister, but he did at least give me a half-hearted hug and told me to behave myself. The nerve of him, indeed!

Mother was actually a little tearful when she hugged the boys, but Papa stoically shook their hands and made them promise to write home at least once a week. They were escorted inside by a prefect, and we departed for our hotel. We were all a little solemn and quiet for a while, contemplating how rapidly life was changing for us all.

CHAPTER 8

After two days in Toronto spent shopping and enjoying the sights, we continued our journey by train to New York, where we boarded the luxury vessel the *Parisian*, part of the Allan Line. Papa knew the ship's captain and the procedures of life at sea, of course. I noticed that Mother was not very enthusiastic about our impending voyage. She never had shared Papa's love of the ocean.

The journey across the Atlantic was remarkably smooth, however, and even Mother eventually enjoyed herself. It was especially pleasing to her to be placed at the captain's table for dinner and to be able to dress in her finest evening clothes. Bowery and I were finding it a bit of a bore, until we discovered that many of the crew were really quite dashing. We both flirted outrageously.

We disembarked at Liverpool and took the train to London, arriving in the midst of Queen Victoria's Jubilee celebrations. Luckily, Papa had made reservations for us in advance at Claridge's Hotel in Mayfair, because London was full of foreign visitors.

Bowery, of course, was greeted by her parents and stayed in their London home. They had extended an invitation to us to also stay with them, and finally it was decided that we would join them on our second week in London. Papa thought it only right to initially allow them some time alone with Bowery after being parted for so long.

I soon realized Mother's delight with this arrangement was that she was achieving the best of both worlds. One week of staying at one of London's most prestigious hotels, plus some time staying with such grand people as Sir William and Lady Maude Bowers. I asked if she would also be looking up her friends Lord and Lady Sinclair while in London, but she promptly dismissed my question.

"Lord Sinclair passed away long ago and there probably will not be enough time anyway," she replied.

Certainly, our days were full for the next month. London was such an exciting place. We saw Indian princes in ceremonial dress and other important dignitaries from around the world, all in London specifically to attend Queen Victoria's Golden Jubilee. We watched the festivities from the terraced balcony of the Bowers home as the Queen's procession headed for Westminster Abbey. This event on June 21st was the first time the Queen had appeared in public since the death of her beloved Prince Albert in 1861, which to me seemed an awfully long time to hide away from her public.

"She's rather a dumpy little figure, isn't she?" I said.

Lord and Lady Bowers both looked at me disapprovingly. Obviously, one was not expected to talk that way about the Queen.

Dressed in black as she rode in an open gilded state landau pulled by six cream-coloured horses, she wore an unattractive bonnet rather than a tiara or crown, which both Bowery and I found disappointing. The crowds cheered her enthusiastically, and she waved graciously as she passed by.

The remainder of our time in London was spent visiting museums, the ballet or the opera, or horseback riding through Hyde Park, admiring the sights. Mother was delighted with it all, but I sensed that Papa would have been far happier back home or sailing on one of his vessels. He was also looking rather drawn and tired of late, and I noticed he sometimes complained of stomach pains. Mother and I fussed around him, and he promised to see Dr. Ralph when they got back to Victoria.

Our time in London passed quickly, and at the beginning of August we headed for the Continent and then to the Sacher Academy in Dresden where Bowery and I would, we were told, be suitably "finished off" on our journey to becoming respectable young ladies.

* * *

Frau Hoenniger greeted us at the door of the academy in stern Prussian fashion.

"Welcome girls. It is *gut* to see you both."

We responded respectfully, but both Bowery and I still had our heads full of all we had seen since leaving British Columbia. We were thinking about the operas, the ballets, the colourful crowds on London streets, the open cafes on the boulevards of Paris, the exotic dining in expensive hotels, the fabulous scenery from the Leipzig to Dresden train, and finally the town of Dresden itself, with all of its picturesque architecture.

Dresden was the capital city of Saxony in Germany and held a charm all of its own. A garden city dubbed the "Florence of the North," its atmosphere was brimming with culture and beauty. For years, Dresden had attracted poets and artists from around the world and taken them to its heart. The carriage that drove us from the train station to the academy passed by the elegant opera house and the royal residence. We also saw numerous artists sitting on the pavement with their easels set up, all creating magnificent paintings as they soaked up the atmosphere of the relaxed gaiety surrounding them.

Frau Hoenniger was a formidable contrast to all the delights we had seen and experienced along the way to finally meeting her, but the academy itself was a beautiful building. The atmosphere inside, however, was somewhat like the Frau—cold and austere.

Frau Hoenniger spoke in broken English, her loud, deep voice grating to the ear.

"Girls," she informed us, "you are here for one specific reason—to learn the art of becoming a lady. You will be taught voice training, embroidery, painting, how to walk with elegance, how to curtsy when required, how to serve tea delicately and how to appreciate the world's finest art and music."

In essence, it all sounded a terrible bore, but Mother appeared to be delighted with our reception by the forbidding Frau and by our accommodations, which I must admit were slightly more elegant than the room Bowery and I had shared at Angela College.

We all took tea in the lounge, where we were offered a small plate of delicate pastries full of cream. Bowery and I agreed afterward that we might easily become addicted to them.

It was finally time to say our goodbyes. Our wonderful European holiday was over and my parents would be returning to Canada. I would not see them for the next two years, and suddenly I felt like a small child again. The only thing that made it all bearable was having Bowery with me.

As we all said our farewells in the garden, Mother took me aside and whispered in my ear, "Sarah, I understand that there is every chance that by the end of your two years at the academy you will be qualified to be presented at court in London before coming home. Isn't that wonderful?"

I looked at her in amazement. "I thought you had to be the daughter of an earl or lord or something to be presented."

"Sir William and Lady Bowers told us that they will be having Margaret presented, and so I enquired as to the prerequisites. It appears that your father's connection with the Hudson's Bay Company holds some merit when it comes to young girls from the colonies, and his standing as a captain is most prestigious."

"But he wasn't in the Royal Navy, Mother."

She tutted and patted my arm. "I know that, Sarah. But he pioneered the waterways of our province as a river boat captain, which is equally important. Just remember what I said, though. There is every chance it will happen, so do behave. I so envy you your opportunities for all of this." She waved her arm in a circle. "The culture, the atmosphere, and especially the music. Oh, what I would not have given for such a chance when I was your age."

For some reason, I suddenly felt empathy for my mother. I understood her passion for music and, although I really had no desire to be presented at court—which in my opinion was simply a marriage market—I realized how much all of this must mean to her. I also had no particular wish to inhale the culture of Dresden, but for that brief moment I had seen in my Mother's eyes a longing so intense that I desperately wanted to please her.

She seemed totally unprepared when I threw my arms around her, just as I usually did with Papa. "I will behave, Mother. I promise I will. And I will make you proud of me," I said.

I swear I really meant what I said, at that moment. But my nature being what it was, it was difficult for me to behave for very long.

And. after all, two years is a very long time.

CHAPTER 9

We soon settled into the routine of life at the academy. We both struggled with embroidery but enjoyed the riding lessons, at which I excelled. I even tolerated the painting of floral emblems on china, and I revelled in the visits to the opera house to inhale all the classical music of Europe. In short, I suppose I was growing up and finally becoming a respectable young lady.

The other side of life at the academy was more relaxed and fun, as Bowery and I discovered life in a European city. Once we had learned how to circumvent the academy's many rules, we were able to escape from its confines on numerous occasions. Consequently I learned lots of things of which my mother would certainly not have approved.

I began to read copiously, not only the required literature for young ladies, but also the more infamous writings of the day concerning suffrage and various women's movements and the role of women in the world. I heartily agreed with much of what I read, for Bowery and I had long ago decided that there must be more to being a woman in the nineteenth century than simply to marry and become an appendage on the arm of a man.

On the other hand, thanks to her continuing correspondence with my brother, Bowery had grown more and more fond of Teddy and in fact vowed her eternal love to him.

"We intend to marry, Bridey, once Teddy has qualified as a doctor. He'll be entering McGill University at about the same time we complete our time in Dresden, and he'll have at least another four years as a medical student. But that won't bother me in the slightest. I will wait for him forever," she declared passionately.

She began to wonder why her parents would even want her to be presented at court. She had no intention of using it as a means to find a husband—the aim of many of the academy girls.

"Oh, Bowery, as we're still so young, perhaps we shouldn't limit our horizons to just one man. It will also be a wonderful opportunity to flirt with so many eligible young men.".

"Yes, I know how much you'll enjoy that, Bridey," she replied drily.

"And after all, Bowery, you always told me there would be many passions in my life concerning men ... so why not yours, too?"

"Teddy is my one and only passion. My parents will just have to accept that."

"But if I am to be 'presented,' you *must* be there with me. I could not bear to go through all of that without you."

"We'll see."

Meanwhile, I continued to absorb the culture of Dresden whenever we could escape from the academy, and this, for me, included flirting outrageously with our Austrian riding instructor, as well as having a brief romance with a German count and a Russian prince, and learning how to smoke cigarettes elegantly. Had Frau Hoenniger known of any of these escapades, she would have been totally mortified.

Amazingly enough, despite frequent opportunities, I did not lose my virginity. I had no idea what I was saving it for. It certainly was not because young women of high morals who came from high-class families were simply *expected* to remain in a virginal state until marriage. To my way of thinking, it was more a case of not finding anyone worthy of giving myself to completely.

I might once have considered Willow a likely candidate. He had inspired in me a great passion, but the men I dallied with in Dresden often turned out to be shallow and uninspiring. The Russian prince, however, was an excellent kisser and taught me the art of open-mouth kissing and the provocative use of tongues, which shocked Bowery beyond words when I related it to her later.

"I really think, Bridey, that it would be safer if you were married, as long as it was a happy union for you. Otherwise you are on the path to becoming a loose woman of very few morals!"

I laughed at her expression, and eventually she laughed too and then begged me to tell her more about the Russian prince and his kissing technique. We experimented by joining our thumbs and index fingers together to make a hole and then sticking our tongues through, pretending they were lips. We always ended up in convulsive giggles.

Finally, in the spring of 1890, we were considered "finished" and miraculously managed to graduate from the academy without too much disgrace. Sir William and Lady Bowers arrived in Dresden to escort us back to London, where Mother and Papa would eventually join us for our court presentation in June.

Sarah Anne McBride, the rebellious daughter of the famous river boat Captain Gideon McBride from British Columbia, had been accepted as a prospective debutante for the upcoming Season. I would now, albeit somewhat reluctantly, enter that prestigious set of marketable young ladies.

I could well imagine the delight of my mother when that particular news reached Victoria.

* * *

"But how, pray tell, are we expected to back out of the room when we have a long train behind us?" I asked our instructor, Mimi, a volatile Frenchwoman who had already successfully coached many young debutantes through this process of becoming ladies of distinction as the wives of wealthy men. All the rules and etiquette involved in being presented at court were quite ridiculous, in my opinion.

No sooner had we arrived back in London at the Bowers' residence in Knightsbridge than we were thrust into preparations for the long-anticipated event. Despite all we had learned at the academy about deportment, we still had to undergo seemingly endless lessons in how to walk gracefully in the Queen's presence. We practiced these elegant walks with tablecloths draped over our shoulders to emulate the long and somewhat cumbersome trains that would be attached to our gowns. In addition, we balanced books on our heads to ensure that we kept ourselves erect and straight-backed.

And then there was the dreaded curtsy! For hours we practiced in front of a mirror to perfect what was known as "the full curtsy." This entailed having one knee bent until it almost, but not quite, touched the ground, a position that had to be held for an appropriate amount of time with head bent.

Then, being sure to keep our balance, we had to rise again slowly without falling over or tripping over the tablecloth train. Bowery and I decided the whole procedure was quite impossible to achieve, and mostly we ended up on the floor, laughing until our sides ached, making our court etiquette instructor shake her head in despair at two such impossible students.

Mimi glared at me at my latest question. "It is quite simple, Mademoiselle Sarah," she replied. "You will simply drape your train gently over one arm, thus, and possibly a page will assist you, but it is imperative that you do not turn your back on Her Majesty, so backing away is essential."

"Oh God!" I said, and that earned me another dark look from the French woman.

And then there were the fittings! We endured days on end of being pushed and pulled into corsets that were tied so tightly we could barely breathe. Our expensive gowns had to be white or a soft ivory color over a completely white background, and they must fit to perfection. We all must wear long white gloves to cover our arms, and the gowns had to be short-sleeved and very low cut, so that a suitable amount of cleavage showed.

In view of the usually strict code of morals that seemed to prevail in upper-class England, this seemed to us rather odd and somewhat hypocritical. Bowery and I thought that it must be because the princes and other gentlemen courtiers enjoyed the view of ample bosoms dipping and bobbing as numerous young women curtsied before their Queen. And the prospective suitors wanted to see what they were getting for their money.

A tulle head-dress, satin slippers, a fan, suitable jewelry, and feathers, completed the ensemble. Feathers were an essential part of the head-dress because Queen Victoria had issued a decree that she wanted to see feathers. Apparently, she was extremely partial to them.

By the time Mother and Papa arrived in London at the beginning of June, I was becoming extremely irritated by the whole thing, but the moment I met them, my mind became occupied with something far more important: Papa's health. I was amazed by how different he seemed since I had last seen him in Dresden. He had lost his robust look and appeared much thinner and paler. At the first opportunity to be alone with my mother, I questioned her about his health.

"Your father continues to have bouts of his old stomach ailment, Sarah, but Dr. Ralph feels it is controllable, so long as he takes his medicine and refrains from eating certain foods. The powders seem to ease the pain. He tires more easily these days, though. But don't worry, dear, I keep a constant eye on him."

"Are you sure it is nothing more serious, Mother?"

She shook her head vigorously, as though trying to convince herself rather than me. "This holiday will do him good, Sarah. Seeing you again will restore his health, I'm sure."

It was true. He did seem to improve as the days went by, and we spent time together laughing and teasing one another. He agreed with me that the preparations for being presented at court were quite ridiculous.

"But we must suffer them for your mother's sake." He grinned. "She is so elated by the thought of her daughter meeting the Queen and being initiated into the court circle."

"But I'll return to Providence after all this is over, so what's the point?"

"I hope you do return, Sweetpea, unless of course some earl or prince happens to sweep you off your feet at one of the court balls."

"That may be Mother's dream, but it is *not* mine, Papa. I will marry for love, if I ever marry at all. And hopefully it will be someone just like you, back home in Victoria."

He whispered in my ear. "And *that* is also my dream, Sweetpea, although he would of course have to be someone pretty exceptional to be like me, eh?"

"Oh, Papa." I laughed. "There will never be anyone quite as wonderful as you."

CHAPTER 10

Eventually *the* day arrived.

Mother and Papa left in a carriage with Sir William for St. James's Palace, where they would be in the audience to watch our presentations. Lady Bowers accompanied Bowery and me in another carriage, acting as our sponsor and chaperone. Afterwards, we would all gather for the reception.

Thankfully it was a warm, sunny day, because we were expected to wait in the queue of carriages outside the palace for some time. Our capes had to be left in the carriage when it was finally our turn to alight and proceed toward the somewhat chilly confines of the Palace Gallery, until we received our summons to the Queen's presence. We were lined up in order of importance of our father's titles. Girls who came from the colonies, such as Bowery and me, were toward the end.

As we each individually approached the Throne Room, we handed our card to the Lord Chamberlain, who pronounced our names after announcing, "A young lady from the Colony of British Columbia in the Dominion of Canada."

My head was, by then, in a funk, and I barely noticed that another gentleman-in-waiting had helpfully spread out my train behind me before I set out across the great room, with my knees trembling and my heart beating much too fast. Bowery was ahead of me because of her father's knighthood. She had performed a perfect curtsy in front of that austere group of royals, the women dressed in their glittering gowns and the men in their uniforms.

Finally, it was my turn to walk across the expanse of carpet and curtsy. Biting my bottom lip in determination and terror, I managed it without disgrace and kissed the Queen's hand before rising again. The royal hand was pale, very small and somewhat podgy. It also felt clammy, which was hardly surprising, because by now the temperature in the room was quite high, and I am sure Her Majesty must have been very tired of repeating this ridiculous ceremony so many times.

Intermittently, a chair was brought from behind, on which she sat for a brief respite. I envied her. I would also have liked to sit down; instead, I gently draped my ten-foot train over one arm as I had been taught and began to back away from the royal presence with as much dignity as I could muster.

It was then that I caught Papa's eye. He nodded and winked at me in a gesture of approval, and at that same moment, a mere ten feet from the Queen, I noticed to my chagrin that one of my feathers had escaped its fastening in my head-dress and was lying on the carpet. Should I bend down to retrieve it? Should I ignore it? The decision was immediately taken out of my hands as a young page leapt out of nowhere and whisked the feather away, allowing things to continue as though nothing was amiss.

I joined the other initiated females on the far side of the room and realized that I had actually achieved the impossible. Sarah Anne McBride had been accepted into high society.

*   *   *

The reception, which consisted of mingling around the large room while servants brought round trays of champagne and other delicacies, continued for a further two hours. It was soon obvious that we were officially entering the marriage market, as various young and some not-so-young gentlemen eyed us up and down as they paraded around the room, stopping to introduce themselves via our chaperones or parents.

Once I noticed Mother and Papa in conversation with a gentleman in uniform across the room. Mother appeared very agitated and had gone quite pale. I pointed this out to Bowery, who asked her mother whom my parents were talking to.

"Oh that's Lord Philip Sinclair," she replied. "He is known to be quite the womanizer. The little dark-haired woman in blue is his wife, poor soul."

"Sinclair? I remember that name. I think my mother knew a Lord and Lady Sinclair before she came to Victoria."

"Oh? Indeed?" Lady Bowers sounded curious and very interested. "I had no idea. Lady Sinclair is quite elderly now, but she still undertakes many charitable functions. Her daughters followed in her footsteps, but the son—well, I hear he was always a problem." She said no more.

I began to be a little alarmed when I noticed that the problematic Lord Sinclair was now heading our way. He had a strange expression on his face that I found somewhat distasteful.

"Ah, Lady Bowers, and your two charming charges," he began. "I understand this delightful creature is Sarah McBride, daughter of Captain and Mrs. McBride, with whom I was just speaking." He took my hand and kissed it in a courtly fashion, all the while eying my cleavage. His lips were moist on my hand.

Lady Bowers sensed my unease. "Yes, indeed, Miss McBride comes from British Columbia. She is a great friend of our daughter Margaret. And how is your dear wife?" she said pointedly, in an obvious attempt to make the gentleman take his attention away from my bosom and release my hand.

"Oh—Mary, yes, she is admirable. Now, Sarah, I hope you don't mind my calling you that. You see, I feel I know you so well."

"Oh, really?"

"Yes, indeed, I knew your mother years ago—little Jane Hopkins. Such a sweet girl she was, and my mother adored her."

Jane Hopkins! I had never heard my mother's maiden name before.

"Yes, my mother has talked of Lady Sinclair."

"Indeed?" He smirked. "And did she tell you in what capacity she knew my mother?"

I was about to answer this somewhat strange question when Papa rescued me from behind.

"Ah, there you are, Sarah! I'm sorry to interrupt this conversation, Lord Sinclair, but my wife is anxious to introduce our daughter to some friends on the other side of the room."

I had a feeling that Papa had been sent over by Mother to rescue me, and I also sensed that Lord Sinclair was not pleased. There was an undercurrent between the two men, and my mother had appeared very distraught when talking to him earlier. I curtsied and made my apologies.

"It has been a pleasure to meet little Jane's daughter—and just as charming as her mother. Amazing that your wife has come so far, Captain McBride. It is quite incredible how one can rise to such great heights in the colonies."

"It is indeed, milord. But only the strong and truly determined people do well—despite how despicably they were treated by some in the old country."

I had never seen my father so angry as he nodded abruptly and took me firmly by the arm to lead me across the room. I had the feeling Papa would like to have hit Lord Sinclair.

"What did he mean by that, Papa? That man seemed so impertinent. I don't know what it was, but I sensed he was being sarcastic about Mother."

"You are probably right, Sarah. His presence here today has upset your mother considerably, because she remembers what a rogue he was as a young man."

"And still appears to be, according to Lady Bowers. She described him as a 'womanizer.' And yet he is married."

"Yes, and has a daughter who was being presented today. His older daughter came out two years ago."

"I wish Mother would talk to me about her past. I would like to hear more about the Sinclairs," I said.

"Well, perhaps she will one day—when she's ready," he replied.

The reception continued, and as time went by my face ached from smiling and my feet, squashed in their tiny satin slippers, grew more and more painful. I was very thankful when we made our escape and returned with the Bowers to their home.

My one thought, as I tried to fall asleep that night, was that at least we only had one more week of receptions and Balls to endure in London, and then, finally, we would be on our way home to Providence. My only regret would be leaving Bowery behind.

But the next morning at breakfast, much to everyone's surprise, Bowery announced her plans to us all. She had talked to me earlier about her intentions, and her parents' permission had already been sought and given. They seemed almost pleased that once again they would not have to be responsible for her care and upbringing.

* * *

"It's true, everyone," said Bowery. "I will be sailing back with the McBrides. Mother and Father have agreed to allow me to live in Montreal with my Aunt Priscilla."

"Montreal?" said Mother. "But why not come back to Victoria with us, Margaret?"

Bowery blushed. I already knew the reason.

"Mrs. McBride, in Montreal I will be chaperoned by my aunt but will be near to Teddy while he is studying at McGill."

Mother looked aghast for a moment, although I am sure she had long suspected an involvement between Teddy and Bowery.

"But, my dear child, there is nothing spoken between you, and Teddy will be so busy with his studies for the next four years at McGill. He won't want any distractions."

"I realize that, Mrs. McBride, and I have no intention of being a burden, but, as I explained to my mother, Teddy and I want to marry once he has qualified as a doctor and—"

"Marry!" Now it was Sir William's turn to look aghast. "I've heard nothing of this. This young chap has not spoken to me. I know he is your son, Gideon, and therefore I'm sure he is a fine fellow, but they are both far too young, and you, Margaret, have hardly seen anything of this young man for the past two years."

"I know, Father, but we have been in correspondence constantly, and I also know we love one another."

"Oh, they *do!*" I added. I also didn't think Bowery should marry without experiencing life a little more, but I enjoyed aggravating the situation and seeing my mother's shocked expression. She glared at me.

"I do agree with you, Sir William," she added. "They are still very young, and Teddy has a long way to go before he becomes established."

"But we will use that time to get to know each other," pleaded Bowery. "It will be a long courtship, but at least I will be near Teddy."

"I think a long courtship, in these circumstances, is an excellent idea," interjected Papa, sensing the growing tension. "We love Margaret like a daughter and cannot imagine a better partner for our son, but they can only get to know each other while living nearer."

"And the courtship will be very circumspect," said Bowery.

"Well, of course it must be!" conceded Sir William. "My sister will be an admirable chaperone, I know. She will be extremely rigid in her demands for proper behavior."

Bowery's mother seemed somewhat downhearted about the whole thing, and I felt sure it was not because her daughter would once again be living across the water. It was simply a case of disappointment, for she had planned a Season for Bowery, during which time she had hoped her nineteen-year-old daughter would snag a gentleman of importance, not a struggling medical student in Canada.

However, she shrugged and patted her daughter's hand. "As long as you are happy, dear, we are happy for you. Your father and I will be staying on in London for at least another two years before returning to Canada, and I will miss you terribly."

"I know, Mother," replied the elated Bowery. She had won her point, and that was all that mattered.

CHAPTER 11

After another boring week of balls and receptions in London, and before sailing from Liverpool in August, Mother, Papa and I took a train journey north to Scotland. Papa had taken my mother to the Broch, his Scottish birthplace, two years earlier on their way back from depositing me at Dresden. This time, he wanted to show me off to his two sisters and their families. I must admit I was excited about seeing the place where Papa was born and where he grew up.

And so, on an unusually hot day in early August, we arrived in the town of Fraserburgh, and I was delighted with all that I saw. Papa said that Fraserburgh had changed considerably since he was a lad, and the herring industry was now a thriving business.

Both Papa's sisters, Aunt Janet and Aunt Fiona, were now widows, having lost their husbands, one to the sea and the other to an ailing heart. They now lived together in a large house on the better side of town, having some years earlier left the village of Rosehearty, where they'd all grown up.

They appeared to be quite comfortable, so the fishing industry must have served them well, although I suspected that since the deaths of their husbands, Papa had also helped them financially. I liked them both immediately, with their broad Scottish accents and warm hugs. They were known in town as the "merry widows," and I could soon see why. They laughed a great deal and thoroughly enjoyed having company. Consequently, the house was always full of visitors, including my gregarious cousins and their husbands and wives.

Aunt Janet had three tall, gangling sons, two of whom were married, and Aunt Fiona had two daughters, both married, with a bevy of offspring. This meant I had five cousins, all somewhat older than me, plus ten second cousins who were more my own age. I had trouble keeping track of them, so Aunt Janet drew me a family tree of McBrides, Ritchies and Buchans.

I also learned more about my grandfather McBride and Papa's Uncle Gordon, who had died at sea during one of Scotland's worst east coast storms, leaving Papa and his two sisters fatherless. I already knew from Papa the story of how he had set off from his village home as a young boy to Fraserburgh to join the Hudson's Bay Company.

We all seemed more relaxed in Scotland. Mother lost much of her stiffness and Papa was certainly enjoying visiting with his family and reliving the past. Meanwhile, I was having fun with my cousins, who took me on many jaunts into the surrounding countryside. Scotland was both wild and beautiful, and I even relished the cold, invigorating winds that blew off the North Sea.

"Aye, she is a wee bonnie Scottish lassie at heart," said Aunt Janet one night as we ate supper together. "A natural—'tis in the blood, Gideon."

"Aye, sister, she is that! Named rightly for her grandmother." They were all silent for a moment, remembering their mother, my namesake, who had died many years ago.

One day we hired a pony and trap and Papa took Mother and I to Rosehearty. He particularly wanted to show us Kinnard Head, where he spent a lot of time as a boy. We took a picnic lunch, and he told us colourful stories of the cruel North Sea, over which we now gazed. I realized his boyhood had been hard, but it had also been full of love, if his doting and affectionate sisters were anything to go by.

After a while, Papa stood up and walked a distance away, to the cliff's edge below the lighthouse.

"He's so happy to be back here, Sarah," said Mother. "It brings back so many good memories for him. Although he never wanted to be a fisherman, he loved the sea, and still does, with a passion."

"I see that. Is this the place where his mother gave him the piece of metal he wears around his neck?"

"Yes, it is his talisman. As he has often told us, he believes it always kept him safe, and it brought him to me."

She paused for a moment as she looked across to where my father stood, and I could see a great love in her eyes. It amazed me somewhat, because my mother was usually not one to show her feelings.

"What about you, Mother?" I ventured, seeing that softness in her expression. "Did our trip to England bring back good memories for you?"

She turned her head slightly and shrugged. "I have never talked about my past to you, Sarah. Just Papa ... he knows everything."

"Was it bad?"

"What makes you think it was bad?"

"Simply because you never talk of it. I have always seen the pain in your eyes, Mother."

She stared off into the distance again, and was silent for a long time.

"How did you come to know the Sinclairs, for instance?" I persisted.

"Ah ... the Sinclairs. I worked for them."

"Worked for them? As what?" I somehow could not imagine my mother working for anyone. She was the very epitome of a lady.

"I worked in service."

"Really?"

"I was Lady Sinclair's personal maid, and before that I was just a scullery maid, and before that ... well, there was the Home."

"The Home?" I was still trying to imagine my elegant and refined mother, who played the piano as though she had been trained by the greatest of maestros, as a *scullery maid!*

"I was an orphan, Sarah. I was abandoned as a baby, just a few weeks old. It was only many years later that I found out about my parents. My mother had had to leave me at a Home called Field House in a village in the Cotswolds, near Oxford. At fifteen, I was still very small but was sent off to work at the country estate of the Sinclairs, and then later came to London with them to their London residence."

"And that horrid man at my presentation? Colonel Sinclair, or now Lord Sinclair? Who was he?"

"Oh that was Philip Sinclair, the son. I never liked him. He was ... dangerous. Anyway, Lady Sinclair, his mother, helped me to escape his attentions. She arranged for my passage to Vancouver Island."

"On the bride ship?"

"The *Tynemouth*, yes."

"Were you one of those sixty women?"

"Ah, I see you have heard about it." She smiled.

"A little."

"Let's not talk any more about it, Sarah. It was a long, long time ago, and I prefer to forget about it all."

"But you met Papa and lived happily ever after."

Her expression changed again and once more she became Jane McBride, the captain's wife, who lived at Providence and fancied herself as someone important.

"Oh yes, we were happy, but to begin with I had envied those who could trace their roots and know they once belonged somewhere. But your Papa also gave me that gift. He found out about my roots. "

"Really?" I nodded, feeling a sudden empathy with her.

"Yes, he found evidence at the Home that I was the daughter of a man called Richard Sheridan, whose parents were a lord and lady. My mother had fallen on hard times after my father died, and she always had intended to return for me—but she died also before she could return."

"Oh Mother, how sad! But I always knew you had blue blood running through your veins. So what of your grandparents. Did you ever contact them?"

"It's a long story, Sarah. My grandmother died shortly after your father found her, so I never met her. She did leave everything to me, though—her entire estate, including her London house, which we sold. It made me quite a rich, independent woman. Ah ... but that's enough for now."

She obviously wanted to change the subject, but for a brief moment I had been given a glimpse into her past. I had seen my mother as another person, the person she had locked away many years ago. But now she was my mother once again, straitlaced and beyond reproach. Although the moment was fleeting, I was glad we had shared it, for I felt that I understood her just a little better now.

CHAPTER 12

We were all sad to leave Scotland, and there were many hugs and tears as we said our goodbyes to my father's family, promising faithfully to visit again soon. I had a strong feeling, however, that my father felt this would be his last trip back to Scotland. The train carried us to Liverpool, where we met up with Bowery and prepared to sail for Canada. It was September 1890.

The halcyon days of my carefree youth were now behind me. Bowery, my dearest friend, would now reside in Montreal with her Aunt Priscilla. After depositing her safely at her aunt's residence, we visited with my brothers at their lodgings in town. They were both about to enter McGill University, Teddy to study medicine and Bertie to attempt business law. They seemed terribly grown up now, and very polished young men, and I could sense my parents' pride.

My brothers even complimented me on finally becoming a "finished young lady."

"I can assure you both that it would take far more than almost three years at a finishing school in Europe and one stupid presentation at court to achieve *that* impossibility," I replied. We all laughed heartily, and everyone completely agreed!

There was obvious affection between Teddy and Bowery, and I realized that their love was indeed strong and would probably endure the trials and tribulations ahead. I was happy for them, and knowing that Bowery would one day become my sister-in-law as well as my best friend made up for the distance that would now separate us.

"I'm really happy for you, Bowery. Truly I am. I shall miss you so much, but in a few years we will become sisters-in-law, which will be wonderful."

She hugged me tightly. "Your time will come too, Bridey. You will meet your one great love, I know it."

And then it was finally time to board the train to carry us back to the west coast, where our long journey would finally end at Providence. I was so excited as we neared Victoria, suddenly realizing how very much I had missed home.

When I saw the beautiful Olympic range of mountains from the city harbour, tears of happiness pricked my eyes. And, to my immense relief, everything appeared the same as our carriage drove through the open gates of Providence a few minutes later. Only one thing was different. There, to the right of the gates, was the cottage that Papa had built for Angelina, looking as though it had always been there. I was sure that Angelina was watching our arrival from a window, or maybe she was already up at the big house.

We continued the last leg of our journey up the long, circular gravel driveway beneath those ancient oak trees and finally arrived at the front porch of the big house.

As I gazed about me, it seemed time had stood still for the past three years, and indeed nothing had changed. I could once more smell the jasmine mixed with the aroma of roses and honeysuckle and was in awe of the beautiful bougainvillea. There was a timeless essence about Providence that would never change.

Immediately, the door flung open, revealing Foo, with Dulcie, Skiff and Angelina close behind him, all of them smiling from ear to ear.

"Welcome home, Captain and Mrs. McBride, and Miss Sarah, my little *menina*," screeched Angelina, with such emotion that it seemed she had feared she might never see me again. Although she was looking older now and her hair had greyed, she seemed as bubbly and effervescent as ever.

"Welcome, Mr. Cap and Mrs. Cap and Missee Sarah. So good to see Missee Sarah. Missed her so much," added Foo.

"Oh, dear Foo, I have missed you, too. And you, Dulcie and Angelina and dear Skiff. It is so good to be home."

Suddenly everyone was talking at once and dogs were barking. Cain and Abel had long since passed on but had been replaced by an energetic golden retriever named Gold and a black and white mongrel named Nelson, both of whom had been puppies when I left but were now large, very active dogs.

And there, standing quietly behind all the noise and confusion, was Uncle Edward to welcome us also.

"Just wanted to be sure that you all arrived back in one piece," he said, shaking Papa's hand and hugging Mother and me.

"My goodness, Sarah, what a beautiful young lady you have become! There will be a bevy of young men knocking down the door now, I fear, Gideon."

"Better not be," laughed Papa. "Or I'll have to get my shotgun out."

"I'm not interested in young men right now, Uncle Ed," I said with conviction. "I'm just happy to be home in Victoria again. I want to hear all the news. What's been happening?"

"Ah well, that would take many hours to relate."

"Well," said Mother, suddenly becoming the chatelaine of Providence once again. "Let's all have tea in the drawing room and we can talk. Foo, would you bring us some refreshments, please? And have one of the maids take up our bags and unpack. Sarah and I will want to freshen up and change later, but meanwhile a pot of tea would go down very well. And Dulcie, dear, I want to talk with you later. We have so much to catch up on."

Dulcie smiled and gave Mother another hug, while both Foo and a new maid scampered off in various directions to attend to their duties. Angelina took it upon herself to shoo the dogs outside, and for a while peace reigned midst all the excitement.

It seemed that much indeed had happened since I was last in Victoria. As we sat enjoying our tea, Uncle Edward brought us all up to date.

"Lady Douglas recently passed away. The city now has streetcars and many new buildings. James and I have added a third partner to our firm, a fine gentleman by the name of Ernest Hamilton who was primarily taking care of our legal matters in northern British Columbia and the Yukon area. He's a bright fellow, Gideon, but a bit serious."

"Something like you were when I first met you, eh, Ed?" grinned Papa.

"I suppose so," he conceded with a grin. "But anyway, the next time he's in Victoria, we'll have to invite him to some McBride/Caldwell social gatherings. Give him a bit of a social life, too, for he works far too hard."

"A good asset to have in your business, though."

"Indeed."

Uncle Edward paused for a moment before asking about Papa's health. "I hope the holiday has done you good, old boy?" he said.

"There has been a remarkable improvement," interceded Mother quickly. "Gideon has experienced far fewer episodes since we met up with Sarah in London. Isn't that so, dear?"

Papa patted her hand. "Seeing our daughter again made me forget my ailments. Yes, I must admit, Edward, the holiday has done me the world of good."

"And what of the O'Reillys and the Trutches?" asked Mother. "How are they?"

Why did I have the feeling at that moment that she wanted to change the subject and steer the conversation away from Papa's illness?

"They are all well. All your friends are anxious to see you back in circulation, Jane."

I pulled a face at Papa, thinking about Mother's interminable "at-homes," which undoubtedly would soon resume.

At that moment, Foo came in with our tea, helped by Dulcie and Angelina, who kept insisting on pinching my cheeks and calling me her *menina*.

So it seemed that, despite all I had seen and experienced in Europe, nothing much had changed at Providence—and for that, I would be eternally grateful.

I was now ready for the next chapter in my life—whatever it might be.

CHAPTER 13

Much to Mother's chagrin, I soon renewed my interest in reading all the material I could lay my hands on about women's suffrage. The movement was growing steadily around the world, and it intrigued me. Mother, of course, told me that such readings were not suitable for young women of my upbringing.

"But, Mother, that is the very reason why I read these books. I have an advantage in life because of Papa's money and position, so why should other less fortunate women have to suffer through poverty? Why should they not be allowed to find positions of work equal to that of their menfolk? Women should be allowed to have a say in the affairs of the world, and even to vote. Why do men think we were put on this earth simply to be wives and mothers and nothing else, when many women have innumerable other talents?"

Mother shook her head. "Sarah, where on earth do you come up with these ideas? The friends you made in Europe must indeed have put some very strange notions into your head."

"Nobody *put* these things in my head. I can think for myself, you know. And, in any event, I simply cannot understand you, Mother. Knowing your own background, I should have thought you would embrace these new ideas."

"My past is in the past. I have moved on."

"Yes, and now you live a good and rich life. *You* managed to overcome so much, so why can't you see that it is important to help others to do the same?"

"I do help others, Sarah, through my charity work."

"Oh yes, a group of silly women sitting around having tea and talking about raising money by holding charity concerts and balls while they embroider—but that's *all* you do. You don't see the complete picture. How the other half actually live and suffer."

"Oh, believe me, I do know how the other half live. So what is wrong with charity work?"

"Nothing—but you just don't seem to understand, Mother. It requires so much more."

"Well, if it means attending those radical meetings one hears about, and becoming militant, I just don't agree with that."

"Mother, I can't talk to you about this," I retaliated. "You simply do *not* understand!"

With that, I left the room in a huff and headed for the stables. I was suddenly very angry, so I saddled up one of my favorite horses without asking the stable boy for assistance, and then rode astride at a gallop across the countryside. Had my mother seen me, she would have been mortified to think that I was not riding side-saddle, in a more ladylike, dignified manner.

Once I was a safe distance from home, I took out a cigarette and smoked it. It gave me malicious delight to imagine the shock there would be if I were to be seen at that moment, and how this juicy piece of gossip would be reported back to my parents.

Sarah McBride was seen riding astride her horse and was actually smoking one of those abominable cigarettes! Horror upon horror!

During the coming year, I continued my quest to better the world for the underdog, and in my pursuit to achieve the impossible, I managed to offend many people, especially my mother. To balance my somewhat defiant behavior, I reluctantly consented to attend all of Mother's social gatherings at Providence. These included dinner parties, picnics, tennis matches and croquet games, plus innumerable boating trips down the Arm.

We also frequently entertained naval personnel from visiting ships in harbour, and I enjoyed flirting outrageously with handsome naval officers, many of whom made proposals to me, none of which I accepted. Most of the proposals were honorable, but I rather enjoyed, and perhaps even encouraged, the ones that were not so honourable. Nonetheless, I refused them all, and did not allow my heart to be touched by any of these dashing gentlemen.

Despite my refusal to commit to anyone, for many months that year, finding a prospective suitor for me remained my mother's top priority. It was really quite amusing how she contrived to invite suitable candidates to dinner and show me off. So it was inevitable that when she heard about a young English architect who had recently arrived in town from England and had won a competition to design the new Parliament buildings, she decided we should invite him along with other friends as a dinner guest to Providence.

His name was Francis Rattenbury and he was about four years older than me. I admit when he first arrived I thought he was quite handsome and very charming. He was very flirtatious and his profusion of compliments even made me blush although I sensed they were not completely genuine. But it didn't take long for me to discover he was also outrageously irritating and argumentative.

I couldn't resist bating him. "Mr. Rattenbury," I said as we began the main course. "I hear you have locked horns with many other business people in town. Is that true?"

My mother raised an eyebrow but papa seemed rather pleased I had asked this question. I sensed that he too had found Francis Rattenbury an unpleasant man.

"My dear Miss McBride," Rattenbury replied. "All geniuses are considered somewhat annoying and will undoubtedly make enemies."

"And you consider yourself a genius?"

"I most certainly have a tendency in that direction."

"My goodness and such a very large ego I fear," I said.

He turned away from me and started a conversation with papa about being a business man rather than an academic. His arrogance was unbelievable.

"I am surprised, Captain McBride, that you accumulated so much wealth without an academic education," he said.

Papa remained calm but by then we could all see how his remarks would easily offend so many people.

I couldn't stand a moment more of his obnoxious diatribe so I pushed my chair back and stood up. "Please excuse me, ladies and gentlemen. I have decided to go to my room where I will not have to listen to more of Mr. Rattenbury's insulting remarks. Good night everyone."

And with that I left the dining room and another of mother's match-making attempts came to an end.

Years later we heard that Francis Rattenbury had taken up with a quiet woman named   Florence Nunn, who apparently enjoyed his behavior—or at least tolerated it and did not complain. They married when she was already seven months pregnant so by then she must have fallen for his so-called charm.

*   *   *

One of the many other visitors to Providence was Ernest Hamilton, the lawyer who was now in partnership with the Caldwells. He was a perfect gentleman, polished, somewhat shy and very knowledgeable about the world. He was handsome, too, in a slightly disarming way, with dark curly hair and a moustache to match, and he was about the same height as me.

In the past, I had always preferred men who were much taller, being overly tall myself for a woman. This fact was minor, though, and only bothered me when we danced, which I began to realize was becoming more and more often. If we both happened to be at the same ball, Ernest Hamilton seemed to take great delight in filling my dance card for most of the evening.

Early in October of 1894, I received a letter from Bertie. My two brothers had just returned to McGill after spending the summer holidays with us and were now entering their final year as students. Bertie was not quite so academically dedicated as his twin, but then, Teddy had always been the better student and the more determined one, and now of course, he was working to achieve his goals not only for himself but also for his betrothed, my dear friend Bowery.

Bertie's letter began as follows:

My dear Sarah,

You will be surprised to hear who I ran into this week. He is taking one of my law courses. He introduced himself as William Baron, but he looked SO familiar, and then I realized that it was Willow, that Indian chap who went to Craigflower School with us! Can you believe it? I asked him how on earth he managed to end up at McGill studying law, and he was quite cautious in his reply. Just said he had a "benefactor" who had helped him. What do you think about that? ... Oh, he's very smart, by the way, and he asked to be remembered to you.

Suddenly I clearly recalled how it felt to be eleven years old again and so passionately in love with Willow. And to think he was now going to be a lawyer, his dream as a boy! I still had a warm feeling for him and was glad he had achieved what he had set out to do, but I was curious how such a thing could have happened. I decided to ask Papa about it.

"Papa, do you remember the boy Willow I went to school with and got into so much trouble by going on a boating expedition alone with him?"

"I do indeed," replied my father as he sat at his desk in the library, smoking his pipe. "Why do you ask, Sweetpea?"

"I've heard from Bertie that he is attending McGill, and studying law! How could that have happened, coming from the background he did?"

He paused for a moment before replying. "I personally kept an eye on the boy, because I had heard he was quite an outstanding student. I talked to Uncle Ed about him when it was time for him to leave

Craigflower, and together we sponsored him for entry to a school in Toronto. The rest he did himself by hard work, and he was able to enter McGill on a scholarship a couple of years ago. He'll go far, I think."

"Oh Papa." I flung my arms around him. "You are such a dear man, far ahead of your time, I think."

"Really?" He raised a quizzical eyebrow at me.

"Yes, you believe in the rights of everyone—whites, the natives, and women too. I think you agree with me that everyone should have a chance in life. That is exactly how I see things. Papa, you would be a perfect speaker at one of our meetings at the Fountain Hall!"

"Sarah, my love, I don't think I am quite that radical—which reminds me, both your Mother and I worry about you going to that place so often. Some of those people are very militant and quite aggressive."

"Oh Papa, not *you* too! I am quite safe, and I would much rather be there than simply passing my time aimlessly socializing over tea and cucumber sandwiches."

He laughed out loud. "Oh, my love, what on earth did your Mother and I create when we had you?"

"What indeed?" I agreed, and we both laughed. I was pleased to see Papa looking so healthy and robust again. It seemed his health problems had righted themselves, and I was most relieved.

CHAPTER 14

In the summer of 1895, my brother Teddy and my best friend Bowery were married at St. Luke's Church-on-the-hill in Victoria. The reception was held on the lawns of Providence, and of course Sir William and Lady Bowers were there, along with Bowery's Aunt Priscilla from Montreal.

Bowery wore a white satin gown trimmed with white tulle and orange blossoms. Her veil fell in folds around her smiling face, held in place by a wreath of orange blossom. Sir William gave her away while her mother dabbed imaginary tears from her eyes with a lace handkerchief.

Once again, I was a bridesmaid, this time attired in a Nile green silk creation, accompanied by three other attendants, twenty-year-old Anna Caldwell and two of Bowery's cousins from Montreal, both of whom were sickly-looking fifteen-year-olds who spent all their time giggling and gazing in awe at my unattached brother, Bertie. Bertie, however, was far too busy attending to his duties as best man and flirting with all the other unattached ladies in attendance.

It was a wonderful day, and I almost envied Bowery and Teddy their obvious happiness. To have found love so young and to have endured this long, I felt convinced it would undoubtedly last forever. We all celebrated with gusto as we offered them our blessings.

The happy couple were to return to Montreal for a year; there, Teddy would become an intern at Montreal's largest hospital, after which he had been offered a very exciting research project in Africa, for which he had applied and been accepted thanks to his excellent grades.

"Isn't it exciting?" confided Bowery, as I helped her change after the ceremony. "After Teddy has completed his internship, he has been offered a position financed by Liverpool University in England. They are hoping to fund a school for tropical medicine research, and it could mean we would travel to Africa so Teddy could research some rare diseases found in human blood. I would be able to accompany him—but, certainly, that is all very much in the future. We hope to return to Victoria eventually, of course, and Teddy will practice medicine here."

"Oh Bowery, what a wonderful adventure. Africa! My goodness. To think my little brother might discover something that would save the human race! But I shall miss you both so much."

"We will write often, Bridey. I will tell you everything in detail."

"Not about the honeymoon, I hope." I laughed.

"Oh of course not!" She blushed. "And soon you will have your own honeymoon. There are so many attractive, unattached men here today that I cannot imagine why you have not given your heart to one of them."

"You always told me there would be many passions in my life, Bowery. I haven't explored them all yet, that's all!"

"You are quite impossible, dear friend! Quite impossible." And we hugged as best friends, for the last time in a long while.

For then the wedding was over and they were gone, and yet another episode in my life had ended. I began to wonder if I would ever find true love myself, or whether in fact that was even what I wanted from life. Was there some other purpose, some other destiny down the road for me?

Two events the following year were to prove that, indeed, my destiny was going to be different from other young women of my generation. Both were shattering and changed my life forever.

* * *

The first happened during the Queen's Birthday weekend cele- brations in May of 1896, observed over four days of festivities, revelry and merry-making. At Providence, we entertained again extensively, with garden parties, dinners and sailing regattas, and the weather remained hot and sunny for the whole period.

Poor Foo and Mary had been completely run off their feet, so Mother gave them both the day off on Tuesday, May 26, to allow them to attend the military festivities held at Macaulay Point in Esquimalt as part of the celebrations. They left early in the morning to head for town and take the streetcar over to Esquimalt.

For once, the house was reasonably quiet, and I was enjoying time in the library with Papa at his desk, going over the books. He was pleased I was showing more and more interest in his companies, now spread throughout British Columbia. By then, Bertie had finished his studies at McGill and was taking the customary year off doing the European tour, but once he returned, it was Papa's intention to hand over the reins to him. It was, however, becoming more and more apparent to Papa and I that my knowledge of his affairs was considerable and I was as good as any man in business matters, even though I might not have the business law credentials Bertie had achieved at McGill.

"I feel confident that when I leave for the Yukon next month you will be able to take over the day-to-day running of events from here in Victoria, Sweetpea. It will give you a head start on affairs, and by the time Bertie returns next year, both of you should be able to take care of things. I shall be gone a few months, as you know. After that, I might consider retirement. Your mother will be happy to hear that, I know."

I smiled. "Thank you for your confidence in me, Papa. I shall enjoy the responsibility."

He handed me a report on a transport firm he had recently acquired in Lytton. "Read this, Sarah, it is most enlightening."

I remember taking the document and gazing briefly at it, and then, in one blinding flash, time stood still and everything in our world changed. An enormous crashing sound, followed by violent and desperate screams made us both look up at once, rush to the window and peer out across the garden towards the water. The sight that met our eyes was horrifying.

"Oh, my God, Papa ... the bridge ... the bridge ... it's collapsed. People are falling everywhere."

Then we heard Mother's voice shouting from upstairs. "Gideon, Gideon, something terrible has happened ... people are screaming!"

We ran to meet Mother in the hall. Then we headed out across the lawn to witness the carnage and horror of that unbelievable scene. A span on the Point Ellice Bridge had completely snapped in half, and a streetcar, some carriages and horses had plunged into the water below. There were hundreds of bodies in the water, and the air was full of long, piercing screams.

Papa, Lum and I went into immediate action down at the boathouse, while Mother rushed back into the house to bring out blankets. Papa and some of our neighbors were taking their boats out into the Arm and pulling people from the cold waters. Without thinking, I pulled off my skirt and, stripped to just my camisole and stockings, dived into the water and dragged back some more people, one of whom I realized too late was dead.

I repeated this four times until, too exhausted to swim any more, I decided I might be more help to the rescued already lying on our manicured lawn.

Soaking wet, I strode up and down in my undergarments. "Did someone call Dr. Ralph?" I asked to no one in particular.

"Yes, there are doctors on their way," I heard someone say.

"Mother!" I yelled. "Bring brandy, and we need more blankets. Some of these people are cold and I think they're in shock." At least we could try to help them before the doctor arrived. Some had bruises and other injuries, probably from being struck by fallen debris.

I remember Mother rushing back and forth, placing a blanket around me too, but I shook it off and laid it over someone more in need. Then I remembered that both Mary and Foo were to take the streetcar that morning. Had they been aboard this one? *Oh God, please keep them safe,* I prayed.

Papa and the other men who had boats kept pulling bodies from the water, and eventually our lawn was covered. I ran up and down the rows of the living, some of them in more distress than others. For some, a small shot of brandy and a warm blanket soon put colour back into their pale faces. Others who had swallowed large amounts of water were coughing and gasping for air. Some needed their wounds bandaged.

I was hardly aware of the other helpers around me, but I knew that we were all doing as much as we could, and eventually Dr. Ralph and his assistant arrived. Just after that, I saw Foo bicycling up the driveway.

"Oh, Foo, you're safe, thank God!" I screamed.

"Went to Chinatown first before catching streetcar, Missee. Oh … my lordy … what a terrible sight … what a terrible sight," he kept repeating.

Mother ran up to him, obviously as relieved as I was to see him. "Where is Mary, Foo? Did she stay with you?"

"She … caught streetcar, Mrs. Cap. Don't know which one."

We paused to gaze around the carnage and horror before us. Could Mary be one of these poor souls? Could she be one of those still in the water, drowned? Or close to death?

I ran frantically along the rows of bodies, assisting Dr. Ralph where I could, covering those who were clearly dead.

The horror continued for what seemed like hours, but eventually we had pulled out all those who could be saved, and the bodies of those who had died were being taken away on carts after being identified by their loved ones. We recognized many of those men, women, and children who had set out for a day of joy and happiness but now, suddenly, were suffering horrific injuries and grief, or worse, had been struck down by death.

Mother was looking at me strangely as we sat together on the front porch later, drinking the cold lemonade Foo had brought us. It was as though she was really seeing me for the first time.

"You were so strong today, Sarah. I am very proud of you." She paused for a moment and then smiled. "And you looked so funny in your pantaloons!"

But this time she wasn't reprimanding me for being so blatantly improper.

We both laughed ruefully. "Yes, I must have looked quite a sight," I said.

"We all did what was necessary."

Foo and Lum, and even Angelina had worked alongside us, as vigorously and dedicated as anyone could have been, but still we had not found Mary, and all our hearts were saddened. We felt sure that if she had caught an earlier streetcar and been across the water safely on the other side before the tragedy happened, she would have got word to us by now.

We knew there were still some bodies in the murky waters, and the search would begin again at first light. We earnestly prayed she would not be one of them.

CHAPTER 15

In the cold light of morning, the true horror of what had happened was apparent to us all, as the news spread like wildfire around the stunned city.

Over one hundred people had been injured, many seriously. It was confirmed that more than fifty people had met their deaths in the murky waters. Six more bodies were dragged from the Arm the following day and, to our great sorrow, Mary was one of them. Mother and Papa had the unpleasant task of positively identifying her body.

There were others among the fatalities that we also knew—a coachman Papa hired to drive his carriages, and many other employees of Papa's who had been out for the day with their families. There were the elderly and there were children. The tragedy had struck the hearts of us all, and our entire city went into deep mourning.

Skiff and Dulcie arrived the next day from Salt Spring Island, where they had been visiting friends. Angelina walked up from her cottage again in the morning, looking exhausted. She hugged Mother and me and vowed her undying support to us. She would, she said, come out of retirement and work for Mother again as her personal maid, and we appreciated her act of kindness, but her age was telling and we knew it could only be a temporary arrangement. She was happy now in retirement as the family retainer in her little cottage by the gates.

The next few weeks were horrendous, as we attended many funerals and helped people who had lost their loved ones attend to legal matters. Many we knew were buried in the cemetery of St. Luke's, while others were buried at Ross Bay. There were numerous lawsuits filed against the city, and Uncle Edward and Uncle James were kept extremely busy. Ernest Hamilton arrived back in town to assist and frequently was a dinner guest at Providence. I slowly grew to admire him even more for his kindness, honesty and integrity.

Eventually the emotional climate in Victoria returned to normal and we began to get on with our lives, though still sickened by the losses we had experienced. Papa began to make plans for his trip to the Yukon, which had been postponed because of the tragedy. One evening a week before he was due to leave, Ernest Hamilton drew me aside and led me outside.

He took my hands in his, and the words that came out of his mouth were not what I had expected at all. "Sarah," he began. "I have already asked your father for your hand in marriage. Now, I am asking you to do me the honour of becoming my wife."

We were standing out on the veranda, taking the evening air after dinner, and I simply stared at him in amazement. Marriage had been the very last thing on my mind that night. And I had no idea that Ernest wanted to marry me.

"I hope I have not shocked you by my boldness," he continued.

"Oh no, Ernest. I am just a little overwhelmed with all that has happened. I can't think of marriage right now."

He took my hand gently and placed it to his lips. "I understand completely, but please at least consider what I am about to say. You have come to mean so much to me, Sarah, and I realize now that I love you deeply. I will be leaving with your father for the north next week, as you know, but will return sooner than he will—perhaps in October, when I will ask you again. Meanwhile, would you do me the honor of giving my proposal your consideration?"

"Oh Ernest, you are such a dear. Your name is quite perfect for you. You really are so earnest about everything. Yes." I laughed at his serious expression. "I will give your proposal my consideration, and will have an answer for you when you return."

Although I detested those silly games women played with a man's affections, I knew that protocol dictated that a woman rarely accepted a proposal the first time it was made.

He smiled as he let out a deep sigh. "I am so relieved that at least you have not given me a definite no tonight."

And so, with Ernest's proposal hanging precariously in the back of my already over-active mind, and with the knowledge that Papa would be leaving for a six-month tour of the north and that Mother would be joining him in a few weeks, as well as the realization that much of McBride's Shipping and Transportation business responsibilities in Victoria would be left in my hands, I faced the challenges before me as July turned into August.

*   *   *

During those first few days following Papa and Ernest's departure, Victoria was hit with an intense hot spell, and we spent most nights sitting out on the veranda trying to keep cool as we fanned ourselves and drank Foo's lemonade. Mother also planned one of her famous dinner parties, and Foo was commissioned to prepare a table of cold cuts and salads to tempt our palates. She invited Uncle James, Aunt Eliza, Joe, Anna and Kit plus the Courtlands, a couple from England she had recently befriended that had managed to infiltrate the so-called elite circle of Victoria.

I remember that night so clearly. And no wonder. It was the night that changed my life forever, because as it turned out it resulted in us having one more guest at our dinner table. It was such a simple occurrence in the grand scheme of things, because we often had additional last-minute guests attending our soirees and dinner parties.

So why, I frequently asked myself afterwards, did this particular unexpected presence have to affect my life so drastically? Why could things not have stayed the same? It would have saved so much heartache.

But it was not to be. Destiny, once again, would intervene.

CHAPTER 16

Beaulah, who was now working for Mother and me as our personal maid, was an exceptional young woman. She was efficient in so many things, especially working on my unruly hair. Angelina had returned to her cottage to enjoy her retirement.

Beaulah was putting the finishing touches to my hair before we dined that night. As I glanced in the mirror, I thought I looked particularly pleasing. My hair was, for once, actually behaving itself in a chignon that she had magically created, simply allowing small curls to escape around my face in cascading tendrils. My skin was unfashionably tanned that summer because I had spent so much time outdoors, but I decided that it suited me. I did not subscribe to the extremely pale appearance that was so popular with most young women of the day. My low-cut dress was of green chiffon, which complimented my auburn curls.

"You look so pretty tonight, Miss Sarah," said Beaulah for the umpteenth time.

"Well, you have created a masterpiece," I replied, laughing. "You manage to do things with my hair that no one else can."

"Thank you miss. Now ..." She looked me up and down for the last time. "I think you are ready, Miss Sarah."

"Thank you, Beaulah. I think so, too."

I left her to tidy up my room as I headed for the staircase. Then I heard Mother's voice drifting up from Papa's den, so I hesitated for a moment by my favourite place on the upper landing. She was talking to a man, but it was a voice I did not recognize. I felt sure that neither the Caldwells nor the Courtlands had arrived as yet, and in any event Foo would have shown them straight into the drawing room. This was a stranger, and his voice was deep and rather sensual. I paused for a moment to listen to their conversation.

"I'm afraid my husband is away on business, Mr. Dupont," Mother was saying. "You have missed him by one week."

"I'm sorry to hear that," replied the stranger. "I was looking forward to meeting the famous Captain McBride."

Mother laughed. "Well, he will be disappointed not to have met you, I'm sure, for your expedition sounds very exciting. Just the kind of thing my husband enjoys. How long are you in town?"

"Only for a month or so, while I organize my plans for the expedition and raise some more funds. It will depend on how soon I can arrange everything."

"Unfortunately, my husband is away for about six months, tying up some business matters in northern British Columbia."

"I see ... well, maybe we will run into one another on some other occasion."

Mother seemed to hesitate for a moment. "Mr. Dupont ... I am sure that Mr. James Caldwell would like to meet you. His father, Edward, has been our best friend and lawyer for many years. Unfortunately, Edward is also away at the moment, on holiday in Europe. His son, James, is in partnership with his father and is dining with us tonight with his family. Please say you will join us all for dinner. He would, I am sure, be interested in hearing about your plans, and may even be able to suggest some sponsors."

"How kind of you, Mrs. McBride, but I hate to impose on a private dinner party."

"Nonsense. Foo always makes far too much food anyway." She turned as I descended the stairs and added, "Doesn't he, Sarah?"

I smiled and nodded and then stared into the face of a man for whom I felt an immediate attraction. Something strange and completely unfamiliar happened to me in that moment in time. I don't know quite what it was, but I felt an immediate stirring in my heart. The man was gazing at me in similar fashion and, for a moment, we were both unable to speak. Did time really stand still, as lovers and poets profess it is apt to do on such occasions?

"Sarah, I was just asking Mr. Dupont to join us for dinner." Mother's voice brought me back to earth. "He came to town specifically to meet with your father on a business matter. Mr. Dupont, this is my daughter, Sarah. Sarah, Mr. Etienne Dupont."

He took my hand, and just his touch made me tremble. When he raised it to his lips, I felt my stomach churn. "I would be delighted to stay, Mrs. McBride," he was saying, "and it is a pleasure to meet you, Miss McBride."

"And you, Mr. Dupont," I finally managed.

There was an embarrassing silence as we both continued to stare at each other. I had never believed in love at first sight, although Papa had often told me that was how he felt about Mother the moment he saw her. But, with my stomach churning and my heart beating far too rapidly, I was prepared to believe anything. For the first time in my life, I was flustered—yes, that was the word—utterly and completely flustered in the presence of a man. It was a feeling I had never before experienced.

Somehow I managed to make my way into the drawing room, and a few moments later the Caldwells arrived, followed by the Courtlands. Foo served some appetizers and drinks before we all headed into the dining room. Etienne Dupont stayed by my side, and we talked briefly of mundane things such as the intense heat Victoria was experiencing, but the way he kept looking at me made my insides turn to jelly. I was annoyed with myself for behaving like a babbling idiot. My only consolation was that I seemed to be having the same effect on him.

Miraculously, we were seated side by side at the dinner table. Anna Caldwell, who was rumoured to be engaged soon to a young naval officer she had met at the O'Reillys, sat to my right and immediately whispered in my ear, "Isn't he dashing? Where on earth did you find him?"

Aunt Eliza smiled benignly at us from across the table, in her usual benevolent manner. She seemed to assume that Etienne Dupont and I were acquainted and that he was my beau for the evening, but Mother soon put everyone straight.

"We are delighted to have Mr. Dupont dine with us tonight," she said as we all sat down. "He had called here unexpectedly, hoping to meet with Gideon and to discuss his expedition to the Arctic. I think you, James, might be interested in hearing about Mr. Dupont's plans. It is something your father and Gideon would have enjoyed investigating."

Uncle James, who had been placed at the head of the table in Papa's absence, smiled at our visitor. "Do tell us more, Mr. Dupont. You have us all intrigued."

I was glad when Etienne Dupont began to speak, because it gave me an excuse to look at him, just as everyone around the table was doing. I could study his handsome face intensely without appearing to be staring. It was a rugged, somewhat weather-beaten face, as though from frequent exposure to the elements. In that respect he reminded me of Papa. He had a gentleness about him, too, and a smile that made my heart crumble into a million pieces.

"First of all, thank you again, Mrs. McBride and"—he turned to me—"Miss McBride, for being so gracious as to allow me to intrude on your dinner party. I had come here on the off-chance of meeting Captain McBride to discuss my plans for an expedition to the north to trade in white foxes. I should mention that, although I grew up in San Francisco with French parents, I left home at an early age to join the Hudson's Bay Company in Upper Canada and spent many years trading for them, until quite recently, when I handed in my resignation and decided to go it alone. I have purchased two schooners; one is anchored here in Victoria's harbor, while the other is back in Hudson's Bay. My intention is to establish some trading posts there, possibly at Chesterfield Inlet and Baker's Lake. At present there is no one trading in those areas, other than the Company, who hold the monopoly, and I hope to become large enough to challenge that situation."

"White foxes?" said Uncle James. "But is there a market?"

"Yes, indeed, the winter before last, over five thousand were traded and another four thousand near to Eskimo Point. They are very plentiful. I hope to have my company up and running by the winter, or next spring at the very latest."

"How are you funding this expedition?" enquired my uncle.

"Well, I spent ten days in Montreal before heading west, where I interviewed many wholesale people, and because of my experience and reputation as a trader, I was able to procure a considerable amount of credit for basic needs such as hardware, gasoline, oil, building materials and so on, providing I paid one-half down and can come up with the balance within one year. I then headed to Victoria to try and raise more money and sponsorship, and I will leave my schooner *Summer Flower* here in the harbour as collateral. I had heard of Captain McBride and his interest in investing in such things. In fact, I believe my parents might have known him from his days in San Francisco, because I seem to recall his name being mentioned by them when I was a child. My father died when I was about ten years old, and my mother passed away a few years later. That was the reason I left San Francisco, as there was nothing to keep me there then."

"I'm sorry to hear that, Mr. Dupont. Yes, my husband lived in San Francisco for a while, as did Mr. Edward Caldwell and James, before heading to Vancouver Island in 1858," said mother. "Gideon and Edward would probably remember your parents, but James was very young when they left there."

"Yes," interjected Uncle James. "I don't remember much of my early life before arriving here in Victoria."

"White foxes!" cried Anna, suddenly becoming animated by the conversation. "How very exciting! Does that mean lots of fur coats and stoles for the ladies?"

"Our market will largely be with the big fur houses in New York, Miss Caldwell," replied Etienne Dupont.

I remained silent for a moment, only thinking of the poor animals that would have to die so that many rich American ladies could wear their skins, but even this did not deter me from my fascination with Etienne Dupont.

"Well, I'm sure that both my father and Captain McBride would be interested in looking into your project," said Uncle James. "Do you have some papers with you?"

"Yes, indeed. I would be happy to leave a portfolio of expenses and all the details of the trading in that area with you for you to peruse and consider. I had intended to stay in Victoria for at least a month ... maybe longer."

Did I imagine it, or did he really glance at me when he added "maybe longer"?

We continued our meal discussing other matters, but I was intrigued by Etienne's stories of his years with the Company. It reminded me of the tales Papa had told us so often, and even Mother remarked on the similarity.

"Your life sounds very similar to my husband's," she said. "He too left home at a very early age to join the Company, and he stayed with them for many years. He headed for San Francisco and eventually for Canada to become his own man."

"And," added Etienne, "I hear he has become quite a legend in these parts."

"Oh, he's quite a legend all right," added Joe Caldwell, who was accompanied that night by his new bride, Emily. Joe and his brother Kit had been mesmerized by Etienne's stories and wanted to hear more as we all headed to the drawing room for coffee.

Eventually, Etienne stood up and said that he should take his leave, offering again his sincere thanks for a delightful evening. He arranged to meet with Uncle James the next morning at his office, to go over all the documentation he was leaving with him.

"You must come and visit us at Providence again, Mr. Dupont," said Mother. "Next time we will show you our garden."

"I would be delighted," he replied, smiling at me. His glance in my direction seemed like an unspoken invitation to so much more, so I responded immediately.

"Mother, the light is still good tonight. It has barely turned nine o'clock. Why don't I show Mr. Dupont our rose garden now?"

Mother looked at me with an expression of annoyance. I knew it was not really appropriate for a young lady to escort someone around the garden alone, especially in the evening light *and* someone we hardly knew. Anna giggled, and the Caldwell boys gave me encouraging looks. They had all seen the obvious attraction between Etienne and me.

But Etienne was the perfect gentleman as he responded most diplomatically. "I would love that, Miss McBride, but only with your Mother's permission, of course."

"Oh ... go ahead, Sarah, but do take a shawl. I think it is finally cooling down a little."

We strolled together across the lawn towards the rose arbour, and I knew we were both very aware of each other. I felt a tingling sensation up and down my spine as we entered the gazebo and he took my hand.

"Sarah ... may I call you that?"

"Yes, of course, Etienne."

"I know I am being very bold, but I must say this to you."

"Please say it."

"I feel something very strong between us, an attraction. But I cannot or should not talk to you this way. We've only just met, and it is far too soon."

"Why not? I feel it too," I replied.

"You do? It seems I have known you all my life; not just for one evening. I must see you again. Please say you will meet me somewhere tomorrow."

"Anywhere." *Was this really me saying these things? It was definitely not the proper way for a lady to respond.*

"Oh, Sarah." He laughed. "You are so impulsive. You know nothing about me."

"I know enough."

He bent over me, his face just a few inches from mine. "In time, we will discover everything about one another, Sarah. You have done something magical to me that no woman has ever done before. What is this magic spell you have woven?"

"Etienne," I sighed, and suddenly his lips were covering mine, at first gently and then gradually, with more passion, to which I readily responded. As his tongue explored my eager mouth, I felt stirrings throughout my body and I knew what we were doing was totally wrong. He was a complete stranger. I was a respectable woman. Or was I? He had inspired in me feelings of wild abandon and passion of which I had never known myself capable. It was indeed magic, and I felt quite delirious.

He was the first to pull away. "You are a temptress, my sweet ... but I must be strong, or else your mother will be very angry with us."

"She would be totally mortified." I laughed. "But then, most things I do mortify her."

"Maybe we should now really take a look at the rose garden." He grinned.

"What rose garden?"

"Ah, Sarah ... you are teasing me."

"Where are you staying in town?"

"At the Driard Hotel."

"Can we meet there tomorrow?" I asked boldly.

"What time can you come?"

"I have to go to Papa's office first thing in the morning, and then I will meet you, say at eleven o'clock."

"We could have lunch together," he ventured. "In my suite?"

"Yes."

We both knew exactly what we were implying, and yet it seemed so absolutely right. Suddenly I heard voices in the distance.

"Etienne, the others have come out on the veranda now. We had better head back to the house, but make it look as though we have come from the rose garden. At least that way our stroll will appear perfectly respectable."

"Oh Sarah," he whispered, as he placed his hand on my cheek and gave me one more quick, gentle kiss. "I fear that nothing we ever do will be perfectly respectable."

I laughed as we walked together back across the lawn toward the veranda, where Mother and her guests had gathered in the fading light. Etienne bade farewell to everyone once again and thanked me for showing him the rose garden. His eyes twinkled with amusement as he spoke.

That night in my room, I wrote a long, impassioned letter to Bowery, which I marked *Personal, For Your Eyes Only.* I knew Teddy would understand because, as best friends, Bowery and I still had private things we liked to discuss. I wrote one page of mundane news and three more torrid, ardent pages describing the wonderful man I had met that night at dinner. I ended my epistle with the words,

Bowery, I have found my final passion at last. This one will last forever.

She would know exactly what I meant, and she would easily recognize the truth of my words, because she knew me so well.

CHAPTER 17

The whole thing was madness and not like me at all.

I was deliriously in love, and it had happened in an instant. I could hardly wait for our appointed meeting the next day. Etienne greeted me in the foyer of the Driard Hotel and discreetly escorted me to his suite. Fortunately, there was no one around who might have recognized me.

We completely forgot about eating lunch as we fell into each other's arms, and many times afterwards I asked myself how it was so easy to love this man. How could I allow this to happen with a man who was a complete stranger just a day ago? I felt no hesitation, and even though I knew immediately he was far more experienced than I in the art of love-making, I gave myself to him without hesitation. He told me he was thirty-three years old, and he seemed very worldly, whereas I was twenty-five and still a virgin and very inexperienced in such matters, despite my European adventures and mild flirtations. This fact initially disturbed him.

"I feel I am taking advantage of you, my love. I did not mean for this to happen," he kept saying as his hands and lips continued to explore my body. "But you are completely irresistible." We were lying together on his bed that day after having consummated our union, and it felt as though we had known each other forever.

"You are *not* taking advantage of me, Etienne," I insisted. "I wouldn't have allowed it had I not wanted this to happen—from the moment I first saw you."

He laughed. "You are quite incorrigible."

"But it is your fault entirely, because you have turned me into a passionate woman who will never have enough of you, Etienne Dupont."

"I have created a monster!" And we laughed and made love again, without thought or care for the future.

One week later, Etienne brought up the subject of what would happen in our relationship in the weeks ahead. Again, we were lying in bed together, both completely naked, with only a sheet covering us.

"Sarah, I love you, you know that, but I also have to leave Victoria in a few weeks."

"I know," I replied.

"But how can I ever leave you? I cannot imagine being separated from you."

"I don't want to talk about it now. We'll think about it when it happens."

And so our mad, passionate love affair continued as August turned into September and Mother began to make plans to join Papa in Quesnel in early October. She had decided to wait until Uncle Edward returned from Europe.

Meanwhile, Uncle James had contacted both his father and Papa and, although they were enthusiastic about Etienne's project and had agreed to possibly invest some money, they were going to wait until Uncle Ed's return at the end of September. Being the conscientious lawyer that he was, he wanted to discuss things with Etienne in person. Papa had agreed to trust his friend's judgment, as he would not be in Victoria himself until December. I was delighted by this delay, because it meant Etienne would be staying longer. I did not want to think beyond that.

Then, one afternoon toward the end of September, while we were out riding together, Etienne reined his horse in alongside mine. "Sarah, let's stop here for a while. It is such beautiful countryside and I want to talk to you."

"Just talk?" I teased.

He smiled his devastatingly handsome smile as we both dismounted and tied our horses to a nearby tree. "Yes, my love, just talk this time."

He took my hand in both of his and we gazed into each other's eyes. Had anyone ever loved this way before, I wondered. Our feelings for one another were quite unique. Incomparable and without equal, of that I was sure.

"Sarah, I want to marry you," he said suddenly. "I cannot imagine leaving here and knowing I will not see you again for months ... maybe years. Come with me, beloved. I know in the beginning it will be a ghastly life for a woman, at least until I get more established on my own, but—"

I placed my fingers to his lips. "Etienne, I would go to the ends of the earth with you, if that is what you want. I love you, too, and yes, I will marry you."

He kissed me passionately. "I have just had a wonderful idea. I want our love to be completely respectable and honourable, so I will delay my plans and stay here until your father returns, so that I might ask him formally for your hand in marriage. We will be married at Christmas, after which we can leave together as husband and wife."

It was the most wonderful idea I had ever heard. A Christmas wedding. I knew Papa would love Etienne too and would give his consent. Even Mother approved of him, although she had no idea we were engaged in such a clandestine, fiery and sexual romance. I had successfully managed to cover my tracks whenever I was with Etienne. The only occasions when we were together that she knew about were when he called at Providence or we all dined together somewhere else.

"Oh yes, yes, yes, it sounds like a wonderful plan. Etienne, I love you so much."

"And I you, my beloved."

It was such a beautiful day, and we were so blissfully happy. For a fleeting moment, I remembered that Ernest Hamilton would be returning in October and I had promised to give him an answer to his proposal of marriage. I felt no guilt, just a slight sorrow that I would have to hurt him, and I vowed to let him down gently. I knew he would understand once he saw how very happy I was with Etienne.

During the first week of October, Uncle Ed finally returned to Victoria, and a few days later my whole world turned upside down and the nightmare began.

* * *

The day after his arrival, Uncle Ed had invited Etienne to his office. When I met Etienne later that day he reported that the meeting had gone well.

"He asked me a great many questions, but I suppose that is only natural," he said. "He didn't seem to remember my parents, though, until I told him more about my mother. Then he asked me a very strange question."

"What was that?"

"He wanted to know when and where I was born."

"Well, you told him you were born in San Francisco in 1863, didn't you?"

"Of course ... but he seemed ... well, for some reason, very interested in that fact."

"I guess he wants to know everything about you, Etienne. Did you mention that you and I had been courting?" I giggled.

"No, I thought it best to allow your mother that privilege."

He kissed me fondly as we parted later, and for the next two days I was particularly busy with matters at Papa's office. Etienne and I had arranged to meet on Saturday at our favorite spot, out toward Cadboro Bay. We always travelled there separately by horse and usually took a picnic with us. It was a very private place, and no one knew we went there. Mother assumed I was still at the office, working on the books for Papa.

In my usual enthusiasm for being with Etienne, I arrived there early on Saturday. An hour later, Etienne had still not appeared, and I grew a little worried, wondering what could have delayed him. It was unlike him to be late. I waited another hour and then reluctantly rode home.

By the time I arrived at Providence, I was feeling despondent. I had not seen Etienne in two days, and I missed him terribly. I wondered if I should take the carriage into town and visit him at his hotel. Maybe he was sick.

While I debated in my room as to what I should do, Beaulah tapped on my door and handed me a letter.

"This was just delivered for you, Miss," she said.

Oh thank goodness. A message from Etienne! I immediately recognized his writing.

"Thank you," I said, anxiously ripping open the envelope.

My eyes read the words on the single page inside, but my head and my heart could not comprehend them. This was some terrible joke that made no sense at all.

Dear Sarah,

By the time you read this letter, I will have left Victoria forever. I apologize for misleading you, but it is best you know now the way that I am rather than find out later. I need to be free and on my own. I can never stay faithful to one woman for very long.

Our affair was pleasant while it lasted, but I will not be passing this way again. I wish you a happy life,

Affectionately.

Etienne.

The world had suddenly gone mad. This could not be true. Etienne loved me. I know he did. I ran out to the landing.

"Beaulah!" I screeched. "Who delivered this letter?"

"A young lad from town, Miss."

"Who gave him the letter?"

"Well, Miss, I don't know that. He just said that two days ago a gentleman at the Driard Hotel had told him to deliver it to Miss Sarah McBride at Providence on Saturday."

Two days ago! Etienne must have left Victoria two days ago!

I ran down the stairs, calling instructions behind me. "I need the carriage, Foo. Right now. Have it brought round to the front."

Mother suddenly appeared from the drawing room. "Sarah, dear, whatever is wrong?"

"I'm going out, Mother. Please don't stop me. I'm going into town."

"But why?" She looked flustered.

"To find out what has happened to Etienne. He must be sick."

"Sarah ..." she called. "Wait!"

But I didn't listen. I had to find out what had happened.

CHAPTER 18

I was already outside and in the carriage before she could stop me. At the Driard Hotel, I rushed through the foyer to the desk and demanded to know if Mr. Etienne Dupont was in his suite.

"Oh, no, Miss. Mr. Dupont checked out two days ago."

"I don't believe you. Show me to his room immediately."

"But Miss, it is occupied by another guest now. Mr. Dupont left on Thursday."

Why? Why! This nightmare could not be true.

"Was there a message left for me here? I am Sarah McBride."

"Ah ... yes, Miss McBride." He looked somewhat embarrassed. "There is no message, I'm afraid."

"But I was under the impression he was staying for a long time. Do you know why he left so soon? Was it an emergency?"

He cleared his throat. "All I recall, Miss McBride, is that Mr. Edward Caldwell visited Mr. Dupont on Thursday morning. It was his second visit to Mr. Dupont, I believe. He and Mr. Dupont talked for a while in his suite, and then Mr. Caldwell left. Soon afterward, Mr. Dupont came down, paid his bill and said he was leaving Victoria for the east."

"What?" I screamed. I spun around, trying to imagine why Uncle Edward had been there again. Etienne had told me about their first visit, and everything had looked so promising. So what had happened, and what had he said to Etienne to make him leave? Had he turned down his request for funding? But why? It made no sense.

I rushed back out to the waiting carriage and told the driver to head for the harbour. My last hope was that the *Beautiful Flower* would still be anchored there. But, of course, it was not. Like everything else, it had mysteriously disappeared.

Mother must know the answer to this puzzle. She must know something I did not know, but I would find it out. I instructed the driver to head back to Providence, but when I got there, much to my chagrin I found the house empty save for Foo, Dulcie and Beaulah.

"Where is my mother?" I screamed at them. By then I must have looked like a wild woman, and they shrank back from me in alarm.

"She left soon after you did, Miss," whispered Dulcie, obviously distressed by my violent mood. "She didn't say where she was going, did she, Foo?"

Foo shook his head. "No, missee Sarah. Don't know where she go. Left in big hurry, too."

I flew up the stairs and thrust open the door to my room, where I flung myself on the bed and read Etienne's note again. How could he have been so cruel? Why had he written this to me? It was only days ago that he had asked me to marry him, and he had made love to me with such passion. This simply could *not* be true! Someone was playing a hideous joke.

The tears came then, in great convulsive gulps, as I lay there scrunching the note in my hand. I must eventually have cried myself to sleep, because suddenly it was dark and I could hear voices downstairs.

I jumped off the bed and splashed water on my tear-streaked face from the basin on my dresser. When I opened the door, I heard voices and realized they belonged to mother and Uncle Edward. They were both in the library. I could see them from my familiar place on the landing because the door was ajar, so I paused for a moment to listen to what they were saying.

Uncle Ed's voice was the first I heard. "So he did send the letter then, as we all agreed?"

"He must have, Edward. Poor Sarah was so distressed when she left. I tried to stop her but .... how did he take it when you spoke with him?"

"Very badly—he did not believe me, of course. I was glad I was able to provide confirmation of the facts."

"Oh my goodness Edward, I would give anything for this not to be true. I truly was happy for Sarah. But thank goodness you asked questions and put things together when he told you about his mother. I remember that lady leaving town soon after I met Gideon."

"Well, Gideon was never in love with her, and once he met you, Jane, well, there was no one else for him. Fleure realized that too, of course, which is why she closed down her business here and left for good."

"Yet she came to you before she left and told you she was pregnant with Gideon's child."

"Yes ... and made me promise I would never tell him. She wanted nothing to prevent his happiness with you, and she promised she would never return to Victoria and make trouble for him. She was a good woman, Jane. I later heard from connections I still had in San Francisco that she had given birth to a son, and a year later that she had married a man called Henri Dupont, who raised the boy as his own."

"And you're sure the dates all coincided, Edward? Could there possibly be a mistake?"

"Absolutely not, my dear. I checked and double-checked. Etienne is definitely Gideon's son."

I felt my head spin, and waves of nausea hit me as Uncle Ed's words penetrated my tortured brain. I had fallen in love with my own ... half-brother.

"Etienne did not want Sarah to know this, Jane. That's why he agreed to write her a letter saying he was leaving her. He preferred for her to think he had deserted her rather than know this about their unfortunate relationship."

"Oh, dear God ... my poor darling Sarah," said Mother.

I rushed back to my room, where I threw up the contents of my stomach from the shock and horror of what I had just heard. Perhaps

I had always known that one day my habit of eavesdropping would prove fatal. That time had finally come. I wanted desperately to make sense of the conversation I had overheard below, but the reality of their words was far too painful. I was simply stunned.

I splashed water over my face again and tried to walk toward the staircase, careful to descend as quietly as possible. Having heard the front door close, I assumed Uncle Ed had left.

Mother was now alone in the library. She had her head in her hands, as if in utter despair.

I broke the awful silence. "So, you decided to arrange my life once again, all nice and cleanly, eh Mother?" I spat the words at her.

"Sarah! Whatever do you mean?"

"I heard it all, Mother. How Great Uncle Ed went to Etienne and told him what he had discovered. Why couldn't you just have forgotten about it? Why couldn't you have kept silent?"

"Oh, Sarah, you know why we couldn't do that."

"Then why not tell *me* first, so that I could decide. No, you always had to run my life for me, didn't you?'

"Sarah, you are bitter and hurt now ... but you will soon realize why it had to be done this way. Etienne did not want to hurt you with this terrible knowledge."

"Instead of which I would have forever hated Etienne, believing he had simply deserted me?"

"Wouldn't that have been better?"

"How could anything ever be better?" I screamed. I paused for a moment before continuing. "Because you see, my dear mother, we have another, far bigger problem to deal with."

She looked up at me, startled. She could obviously not imagine anything worse than the terrible knowledge of a relationship between siblings.

"This incestuous relationship between Etienne and I that you were so desperate to hide and make go away, will never, ever go away, because I discovered last week that I am expecting a baby. I was going to tell Etienne today. We had planned on marrying at Christmas anyway. Imagine that! You always love to organize everything and everyone, so now you can sit there, Mother dear, and try and work out how you are going to manage that!"

Mother gasped as I left the room and slammed the door behind me.

PART TWO

The Aftermath

JANE
(1897-1899)

CHAPTER 19

After she left, I relived the nightmare of those horrific hours that had followed Edward's return to Victoria.

I had told Edward about our dinner guest and suggested they meet to discuss his request for finances before Gideon returned. He had agreed. But later, Edward came to me, hinting at a terrible discovery he'd made. At first he was reluctant to share the details, but I pressed him on it because he had looked so troubled.

"Jane, I hate to tell you this, but I have put together all the facts he gave me about his childhood in San Francisco and what I already knew."

"Whatever do you mean?"

He then told me about Fleure, a friend of Gideon's from long ago, and why she had left Victoria. I felt numb. Etienne was Gideon's son! Neither of us could believe this terrible twist of fate that had brought Gideon's son to our city, and into the heart of my daughter.

"Edward, if you are absolutely sure of this," I said, "I think you should go back to Etienne and tell him. I know he is very fond of Sarah ... romantically."

Edward returned to the Driard the next morning and handed Etienne the papers he had as proof of this terrible knowledge. There was a record of his mother's departure from Victoria and a short note she had written to Edward soon after, telling him that she had settled back in San Francisco. In April of 1863, she had sent another short letter telling of Etienne's birth. They had not been in correspondence since then, but Edward had heard through friends of her marriage to a Henri Dupont. At first, Etienne had continued to insist that Henri Dupont was his father.

But Edward had persevered with the truth, and with the documents now before him, Etienne eventually came to believe this terrible nightmare. Edward then suggested to Etienne that he write a letter to Sarah, telling her he was leaving Victoria for good. Etienne finally agreed that he would and then have the letter delivered after he had left town. He said he would rather her think badly of him than to know this unspeakable truth.

But then, on the following Saturday night, long after Etienne Dupont sailed out of the harbour aboard the *Beautiful Flower*, Sarah had overheard my conversation with Edward in the library. And now she knew the whole truth—and had the added burden of her pregnancy.

With all that happened during those hours, I had had no time to consider my own feelings about Gideon having another son. As a young woman, while I had had two miscarriages, and suffered the death of our first son in the early years of our marriage, would it have helped him to know he had another healthy son by another woman—a woman who had put her own feelings for Gideon aside and allowed him to be happy with me? Edward promised never to let Gideon know.

I was not so naive as to imagine Gideon had not been involved with other women before we were married. He had seemed far too experienced and virile a lover, but the thought of another woman bearing his child was very different and hard to accept! After all those painful years of being childless and then losing our son, I now was carrying this knowledge that he did in fact have another son with that other woman. I recalled meeting Fleure on the street that day in Victoria. She had seemed so nice, but her eyes were sad. Now I understood why.

Would it be a mistake to tell Gideon about this now? It would do no good, anyway. In any case, I couldn't allow myself to think about it right now, because I was so consumed with the pain my daughter was suffering. My heart was weeping for her.

* * *

I had survived many turbulent episodes in Sarah's life before this one.

I thought back to her daring escapades as a child gallivanting with native children; her determination to undertake dangerous pursuits in an unladylike fashion; her refusal to study her lessons; even her threats to become an actress. I had tolerated her refusal to be moulded into a well-behaved young lady, even after being tutored at a finishing school in Europe and later a presentation at court in London, and I had always tried desperately to understand her wild streak and her desire to save the world! I knew she had a free spirit within her that undoubtedly would never be completely tamed.

In truth, I had understood her a little more while watching her care for those poor, wretched souls that fell from the bridge on that tragic day in May. Her compassion for them had touched my heart.

And when Etienne Dupont came into her life this summer, I saw in him a man of strength who could perhaps be her equal. I was happy for her, I swear I was, and I felt sure that when Gideon returned he would also approve of Sarah's obvious love for this man.

But then this terrible truth had come to light that I knew would rip my daughter's heart apart, and I was powerless to prevent it. Why, of all the men in the world, did she have to fall in love with this one?

And now this shocking and completely unspeakable announcement she had just made was beyond anything I could ever have imagined. It was not simply that I was dismayed by the fact of my daughter's pregnancy, which proved she had been involved in an immoral way with him. That I could have accepted, for I had long ago reconciled myself to the possibility that Sarah might be intimate with a man before marriage. She was always so flirtatious, and it was bound to encourage her suitors. No, it was not just a moral issue. It went far beyond that.

In this particular situation, the very thought of intimacy was appalling, repellent and nauseating—an unspeakable situation too frightful to comprehend. As I looked into my daughter's beautiful eyes and deathly white face, I saw the same horror there that I was experiencing. But I felt an enormous sorrow for her, so great and full of heartache that I wanted to take her in my arms and erase the mental anguish she must now be feeling. I wished that I could have held her, but she had rushed past me so quickly, slamming the door behind her as she headed out into the night.

I sensed she needed to be alone, and I suspected she would go to the garden gazebo or down to the boathouse, to sit by the water and think. But oh, what horrific and heinous thoughts she must be having. If she ran to the water's edge, I prayed she would not feel as desperate as I had once felt, after Caleb died. Surely, surely she wouldn't try to kill herself.

I blamed myself. If only I had not invited Etienne Dupont to dinner on that fateful night. I should have just sent him on his way, and Sarah and he might never have met, and he would undoubtedly have left Victoria long before Gideon's return.

If only—but it was far too late for such regrets now. Far, far too late.

Whenever facing problems, I had always turned to Gideon for love and support, trusting that somehow he would find an answer for me, but that wasn't an option in these circumstances. Although I had vowed never to lie to Gideon again, nor keep things from him, I decided it was best that Gideon never learn of this. It was enough that Edward and I knew of their relationship ... but a child? Oh, dear God, how could that ever be explained or dealt with?

In other circumstances, Gideon would have had the right to know of Etienne's existence, and I was sure he would have been proud of the man his son had become. But he must never, ever know now, because he would then also discover that this was the man who had fallen in love with his daughter and that, between them, they had produced a new life.

My thoughts were too unbearable to comprehend. My head ached, and I knew I needed to lie down, so I left the library and headed upstairs to the private sitting room adjoining my bedroom. I lay down on the sofa and tried to rest, but my brain was filled with wild, unthinkable thoughts. I got up again and headed for the spiral staircase leading to Gideon's turret at the top of the house. Maybe up there I could find some semblance of peace. I lit the small gas lamp and stared out at the darkness below. Somewhere out there in the garden or down by the water, my darling Sarah was suffering.

Oh Gideon, what am I to do? How can I help her?

* * *

At least an hour must have passed before I heard the front door open and then close and her footsteps coming slowly up the stairs. She tapped lightly on my bedroom door before entering.

"I'm up here, Sarah," I said, "in the turret."

"I know. I saw the light," she called back as she climbed the stairs to where I sat.

She looked dreadful. Her hair was in wild disarray, her face still a deathly white and tear-streaked, but her expression was now both formidable and determined.

"I've made a decision, Mother," she said quietly.

"Ah ... Sarah ..." I tried to touch her hand, but she shook me off as she sat in the chair opposite mine.

"This is the way it is has to be. Ernest Hamilton proposed marriage to me before he left for the north. He is expecting an answer from me when he returns next week. I have decided to accept his proposal."

"But ... Sarah."

"Wait, Mother! I will only accept his proposal *after* I have told him about the child I am carrying. I will *not* of course tell him of my ... exact relationship ... to Etienne. I will simply tell him that I had a brief affair and that the man deserted me. If Ernest still wants to marry me, knowing of the existence of the child, I will agree to a speedy wedding date, on the understanding that the child will be raised as his. For all intents and purposes, people can assume that Ernest and I had a relationship before marriage, because obviously the baby will be born early. I estimate it will come in late May or early June of next year. I will suggest to Ernest that, with Papa's approval, we can be married in December, perhaps on my birthday, or sooner if everyone agrees."

"Do you imagine that Ernest will agree to that?"

"He loves me, Mother."

"Yes, but ...."

"Well, if he doesn't agree, and I wouldn't blame him if he didn't, I will still have the child, but I will go far away to avoid you any embarrassment, maybe to Montreal and be with Teddy and Bowery ... or even to Scotland. I could stay with my aunts and cousins there and say that I was widowed, whatever would make this whole miserable situation respectable again."

"These are definitely possibilities, Sarah, but ... the baby? I still wonder ..."

"Wonder what, Mother? Whether it will be born with two heads, or a missing limb? After all, it will be the result of an incestuous relationship, right?"

"No, Sarah, I didn't mean that! I just meant that it will be difficult for you to raise a child without a husband."

"Well, Ernest might still agree to marry me. Who knows? He is a good man."

"Yes, he is," I said lamely.

"But I have some conditions attached to these plans, Mother," she continued.

"Conditions?"

"Yes, if Ernest does still want to marry me, even Uncle Ed, who knows about Etienne being Papa's son, must *not* know that I am pregnant right now. He too must be under the impression, when the time comes, that the child is Ernest's. Is that clear? Papa, too. Everyone, in fact. Only you and I will know the baby's true parentage. Ernest of course will also know it is another man's child, but he will not know about Etienne and our sibling relationship. No one must know that! Ever!"

"Of course, my dear. It is just between you and me ... but how will we explain to Papa that Etienne Dupont has left town and no longer wants investment in his trading venture? Your papa is expecting to meet him."

"Uncle Ed must tell Papa that Etienne raised all his funds and left abruptly. I hope you have not already written anything about Etienne and me to Papa."

"No, not really. Just that you seemed to get along well."

Sarah digested this in silence, and then said sadly, "Yes, yes, we did. It seemed so perfect, Mother, and yet it was so terribly wrong. How could that be?"

I shook my head, my heart breaking for her in her distress. I had no answers, so I simply said: "I will stay here now at Providence with you until Papa returns. Perhaps I will even ask him to come back a little sooner. Certainly, if Ernest still wants to marry you, we will have a wedding to plan."

"Yes, Mother," she sighed. "We will have a wedding to plan. Everything must be perfectly respectable!"

Her tone was sarcastic now, but I did not retaliate. I understood how she must feel. "And if Ernest decides he does not want me and my child, then you can explain to Papa, and only Papa, that I am going away on a long trip."

"Sarah, it may not come to that. I pray that it doesn't."

"I have stopped praying, Mother. If there were a God, He would not have allowed this terrible nightmare to have happened in the first place."

She turned and left the room, and something in the coldness of her manner reminded me of myself, so long ago, when I was torn apart by losses too hard to bear and I had allowed an insidious layer of ice to invade my heart and almost destroy my life.

Oh, Sarah, please don't let that happen to you too, I begged inwardly

CHAPTER 20

A week later, Ernest Hamilton returned to Victoria.

After reporting on business matters at Caldwell, Caldwell & Hamilton, he immediately sought out Sarah at Providence. We were all very formal and polite to one another in the drawing room as Foo served us tea. Sarah seemed to be avoiding being alone with Ernest, as though putting off the inevitable confrontation with him. I knew she understood she had to follow through with her plan as quickly as possible, and Ernest was obviously eager to have her reply to his proposal. He spent the entire time gazing lovingly into her eyes, barely aware of my presence.

"Maybe you would like to join us for dinner tonight, Ernest," I said, thinking this would help Sarah and give her a little more time to prepare. Then, perhaps, after dinner, they could spend time alone on the veranda. The evenings were still quite warm, as we were experiencing an Indian summer that year.

"I would be delighted, Mrs. McBride," he replied.

"Dinner will be at seven," I said. "Do come a little earlier for drinks. Edward and James and the Caldwell brood will also be here."

He looked alarmed, until Sarah interrupted, "I'm sure we will find some time alone, Ernest." She smiled at him, and perhaps only I could see a coldness in that smile reflected in her eyes. I realized then that she knew what she had to do, and being the strong person she was, she would do it.

Dinner was reasonably pleasant. There was the usual laughter and hilarity that always occurred whenever we were with the Caldwells. No one, other than Sarah and I, sensed any underlying tension.

Then Joe's wife, Emily, announced they were expecting a baby the following summer. She was radiant, and Joe looked the picture of the proud father-to-be. I joked with Edward about being a great-grandfather, and James now a grandfather. I sensed that Sarah's heart was breaking and she wanted to escape. And then Anna gave us her news concerning her beau, the handsome naval captain.

"Robert has asked Papa for my hand in marriage," she said, beaming. "We are to be married in the spring."

Everyone muttered their congratulations, and toasts were made to the future bride and groom and to the coming baby.

"It's so wonderful," added Anna. "I will be a bride and an aunt all at once."

Suddenly Sarah stood up, made her excuses and said she was going outside to get some air because of a headache. Ernest immediately took his cue and was by her side in an instant.

"I will walk with you, Sarah. Maybe the fresh air will do you good."

She smiled weakly. "Yes, Ernest, please do."

They were gone for a very long time. Dinner was over, and Foo had served us all coffee in the drawing room before the front door opened once again. The men had just been on the point of retiring to the library for port and cigars, but they were stopped in their tracks by the sight of Sarah and Ernest, who stood holding hands in the doorway and smiling at everyone.

Sarah spoke first: "Although Papa has not given his official approval, I am sure that he will, just as I know you will also, Mother. I have just accepted Ernest's proposal of marriage, and we are to be married before Christmas."

Everyone gasped.

"Goodness!" said James. "What a night! This is wonderful. All these engagements and birth announcements. I don't think I can stand any more excitement."

"Well, don't worry about me, Father," Kit said, grinning. "I'm a confirmed bachelor."

We all laughed as we congratulated Sarah and Ernest and more toasts were made to their happiness.

"Oh, Sarah," cried Anna. "Could we not make it a double wedding in the spring? Wouldn't that be wonderful?"

Sarah smiled weakly. "It's a lovely idea, Anna, but Ernest and I have known each other a long time now, and we are anxious to start our life together as soon as possible. With Papa's approval, we hope to marry before the end of November—if he is home by then."

This was my cue. "Well, dear, I will write to him at once and tell him the news. I am sure he will return immediately, now that we have a wedding to plan."

Edward looked across the room at me with raised eyebrows. I knew he was puzzled, and my suspicions were correct when he later cornered me and whispered, "Sarah seems to have recovered from her feelings for Etienne very quickly, doesn't she, Jane? Am I right? Or is this a rebound thing?"

He did not appear to suspect other reasons for her speedy wedding arrangements, so I replied as calmly as I could: "Edward, I have never completely understood my daughter, as you well know, but I do know she was very fond of Ernest ... even before she met Etienne, and maybe she could see he was by far the better man. He is much more stable and reliable, and he certainly appears to adore her."

"With that I heartily agree," he replied.

When everyone had left that night and Sarah and I had retired to our rooms, I slipped along the corridor and tapped on her door. She was sitting by her mirror, and Beaulah was unpinning her hair.

"Hello, Mother," she said brightly. "Come for a bedtime chat?" Although her voice was cheerful, there was still that underlying sarcasm.

When Beaulah took her leave, I sat down on the edge of the bed.

"He accepted the situation, then?" I asked.

"Yes, Mother, he still wants to marry me ... despite everything. He is quite a remarkable man. He didn't even demand to know the details or who the cad was who had left me in the lurch, so to speak."

"He is indeed a kind and loving man, Sarah."

"And very forgiving."

"Yes, indeed."

"But he insists that the child is thought of as his, and his alone. He specifically asked me if anyone else knew that I was pregnant ... even my lover?"

"And what did you tell him?"

"I lied, Mother. I had to. I told him that no one knew. I said that he was the first to be told because I had only just discovered myself, and my so-called 'lover' had no knowledge of the child, which is true. I also said he would not have married me even if he had known, because he had long since left Victoria."

"That is best, Sarah. It will just be between you and me, and I will never mention it again. The child will be raised as Ernest's as far as I am concerned."

"Thank you, Mother."

She stood up and came towards me. For a moment I thought she was about to put her arms around me, but she hesitated and the moment passed, and she merely turned down her bed instead. "I'm very tired now. I think I'll try and sleep."

I stood up, too. "And I will write to Papa and tell him that you and Edward wish to be married as soon as possible. I am sure he will return earlier than planned, especially when I confirm that I will not now be joining him in the north."

She nodded and then lay down on the bed. I stood for a moment looking down at her and then bent down to place a kiss on her cheek. I wondered, for a moment, why I had not done that more often. She so desperately needed my affection.

Her reaction was to smile up at me and say, "Thank you, Mother," before closing her eyes in an attempt to shut out the nightmare she had been living.

CHAPTER 21

I wrote a long letter to Gideon that night, telling him of all the developments that had taken place within the Caldwell and McBride families. Mostly I talked of Sarah and Ernest's announcement that they wished to be married as soon as possible.

For this reason, Gideon, I am hoping you can tie up your business as quickly as possible and come home. I feel now I should not join you this month as we planned, as there will be many preparations to make for a late November or early December wedding! Sarah and Ernest are both anxious to have your approval.

There will be much to be arranged. They seem so much in love and I want nothing but Sarah's happiness.

I felt I had to add the last part, even though I knew there was not the same passion in Sarah's eyes for Ernest that I had seen there when she spoke of Etienne.

Within two weeks, Gideon's reply arrived:

My beloved wife,

Good heavens! Whatever next? I knew that Ernest had proposed to Sarah because he spoke to me about her when he was up here with me. But then you mentioned in one of your letters some other fellow that had arrived in town—Etienne Dupont, wasn't it? The same fellow who wanted Edward and me to invest in his Hudson's Bay project?

You said that Sarah and he seemed to be getting along very well, and I imagined that Sarah would surprise us all and fall for this adventurer. What happened to him? Anyway, I am delighted now that she and Ernest want to marry. He seems a very good and honourable man.

Yes, my dear wife, please don't come north now. The winter is settling in early and I have just about completed all that I wanted to do to tie up the loose ends so that next year I can retire and hand over the reins to Bertie—if he ever returns from his travels through Europe!

So, I should be leaving Quesnel next week and will be back in Victoria before the 1st of November. I cannot wait to see you again. I have missed you so much and long to be with you again, my love.

Tell the happy couple that they have my approval and blessing, and can go ahead and set a date any time in November.

I sighed with relief. Everything was going ahead as planned. I wrote back joyously.

My beloved Gideon,
I am thrilled that you will be home soon. I have missed you so much too, more than you will ever know.

The brief attraction between Sarah and that fellow you mentioned did not last and, having raised all the funds he needed (as Edward will explain to you,) he left Victoria some time ago. He appeared to be a nice enough man, but he led an extremely undisciplined life and seemed to enjoy his travels and would never have settled down. Ernest is far better husband-material and much more reliable. I am sure he and Sarah will be very happy together. They have chosen the last Saturday in November, the 28th, to be their wedding day, and the ceremony will take place at St. Luke's. As it's a winter wedding, I hope we will be able to accommodate all the many guests for a reception inside Providence.

I felt I owed Gideon some explanation concerning Etienne Dupont because I had mentioned the earlier attraction I felt was happening between him and Sarah. Having written those words, I considered the matter to be closed and I prayed that we would now all be able to go on with our lives happily. This was something I would never be able to share with Gideon, but I hated having to lie by omission. I knew from past experience how easily lies can come back to haunt you. But I knew I could never tell him that Etienne Dupont was his son. It still hurt me to think that he was, but he must never know that Sarah was carrying his child.

I closely watched my daughter in the days before her father arrived, and I worried about her. She seemed to be moving in a trance, doing all the things a bride-to-be was supposed to do, smiling when expected to smile, giving the appropriate answers to questions, and attending fittings for her spectacular wedding gown, but deep within her was an incredible sorrow, a sorrow that only a mother who knew the true story could detect.

Gideon arrived in Victoria at the beginning of November, and I was immensely happy to see him again. One week later, much to our great delight, Teddy and Margaret also arrived from the east. Sarah had asked Margaret (or Bowery, as she still insisted on calling her) to be her matron of honour, but we did not expect they would be able to come so soon. Teddy, however, had completed his internship in surgical pathology and general medicine in record time at the Royal Victoria Hospital in Montreal. The following year, he would be heading for the Liverpool School of Tropical Medicine in England on a scholarship he had won, to prepare him for his research tenure in Africa.

I must admit I was concerned when I first saw Margaret. She was so pale and thin and did not look at all well. Eventually she told us the reason. A month earlier she had suffered a miscarriage, and Teddy had deemed it wise to bring her to Providence for a long rest. I fully understood the depth of her suffering and was glad they planned on staying until the spring, which pleased us all. If all went well, they would be heading for Liverpool in the spring or early summer, after tying up things in Montreal.

We were excited to have them with us, and I knew that Sarah would benefit from her sister-in-law's presence. They talked together for hours on end, but I was never completely sure if she had confided in Margaret about the expected baby and its father. I thought it best not to ask, and maybe Sarah had decided to not even mention it, in view of Margaret's own loss.

"Are you sure you will still be able to be my matron of honour, Bowery?" I heard her ask Margaret one morning. "Do you think you are well enough?"

"Of course, Bridey! What a question! I wouldn't miss it for the world!"

Sarah's other attendants were to be Anna Caldwell, Gertrude Rithet and Kathleen O'Reilly. Kathleen would herself be departing for Ireland directly after the wedding to be presented to Lord Lieutenant and Lady Countess Cadogan in Dublin.

Soon, Providence was a flurry of activity as seamstresses arrived in droves to fit the girls in their gowns, and preparations were made for the enormous wedding banquet we planned following the ceremony. Foo, Dulcie, Beaulah and Angelina all considered themselves to be in charge of arrangements, but I felt confident that Foo would win the final battle for superiority.

It seemed that everyone of importance was coming to what was turning into a most auspicious event. The famous Captain McBride's daughter was to be married, and it was the talk of the town. Sarah did not seem to object to all the extravagant arrangements; in fact, she rather encouraged it, as though trying desperately to obliterate her feelings for Etienne and emphasize the importance of her marriage to Ernest. During the days leading up to her wedding, I must admit, I prayed a great deal. I was determined to make her day a happy one, and I vehemently hoped that her future with Ernest would turn out well.

Two days before the wedding, we received a telegram from Bertie, who was still in Paris. It read:

Desperately sorry not able to be with you. Stop. Can't believe a man has finally tamed you, sister dear. Stop. My best to Ernest and undying brotherly love to you, Brat. Stop. Hope to return in the Spring. Stop. Will bring a surprise for you all. Stop. Bertie.

We were all disappointed not to have Bertie there, and I was slightly irritated by his lack of effort to return for his sister's wedding. I also dreaded another *surprise*, whatever it might be. Could I stand anything more, I wondered?

November 28 finally arrived, and with it came Victoria's first light dusting of snow. We awoke to a brilliantly beautiful morning, sun shining on a sparkling white world of recently fallen snow. I hoped it was a good omen.

As Sarah descended the staircase to be greeted by her father in the foyer, I gazed up at her in wonder. She had truly never looked more beautiful. Her dress, designed by the London House of Worth and made in record time by one of Victoria's most proficient seamstresses, was of white and silver brocade with a long train brocaded in silver. Her veil and trimmings were made of Honiton lace, and she carried a cascading bouquet of wild pink roses. Her attendants, following behind her, wore pale apple-green silk gowns and carried posies of miniature white roses.

I heard Gideon gasp in awe at the sight of his daughter. His gaze, which had been focused on my portrait at the head of the stairs, quickly went to Sarah as she appeared. He stared at her intently before turning to me and whispering, "She is just as beautiful as her mother. How could I have been so lucky as to have two such beautiful women in my life?"

"Oh Gideon ..." I said, but my breath was also taken away. Sarah was spectacular, but the words *ice maiden* also came to mind. She descended slowly in a majestic manner, her lips quivering slightly as they turned into a small smile when she placed her hand in Gideon's.

"Well, this is it, Papa. I'm ready to be thrown to the lions," she said, and we all laughed.

"Ah, Sweetpea, the lions will gaze at you in wonder, for you are indeed a bonnie lass," replied her father.

Teddy and I drove ahead to St. Luke's in the first carriage, followed by Sarah's attendants in the second. The third carriage brought Gideon and Sarah. An entourage consisting of Foo, Dulcie, Skiff, Angelina, Lum and Beaulah had already walked up the hill to the church, and all the other guests, including the many Caldwells, were waiting inside.

I often wondered what Gideon and Sarah had said to each other when they were alone. Whatever it was, my husband had somehow imparted courage into his daughter's heart, for when she arrived at the altar to pledge her life to Ernest, she seemed calm and resolute.

Later, at the reception, Sarah whispered to me on the side, "It is still just our secret, Mother. I have told no one else—not even Bowery."

"I'm glad, Sarah. It will always remain that way, I promise. I pray for your happiness, dear."

"Thank you, Mother," she whispered again. "I think I truly will be happy with Ernest. He is so very kind."

I smiled at her, but my heart was inwardly saying: *Kind?* I knew my daughter needed *passion* in her life. She was not like me. I had been content to marry her father because he was a kind and loving man, and I had been lucky, because I had grown to love him through the years with a wild passion.

But Sarah? Would she ever be content with just *kind?*

As we waved them off on their honeymoon later in the afternoon, my emotions were mixed.

CHAPTER 22

That night, as Gideon and I prepared for bed, he had another dreadful stomach pain, which, for a moment, made him double over in agony. I was terribly concerned and said I would have Foo go for Dr. Ralph at once, but as soon as the pain had passed, Gideon insisted he was fine.

"I will take my powder, dear," he said, as I bustled around preparing his dosage. "This is the first episode in a long time. I really feel it is nothing ... just the excitement of the day."

And indeed that appeared to be the case, because there was no recurrence in the coming days or weeks.

Christmas that year was a special joy. Our house was full of loving family members, and I had never felt so happy and secure about our future. Sarah and Ernest had returned from a short honeymoon in New Westminster and were talking of building a house on land that Ernest had purchased in the Rockland area. Meanwhile, they were occupying the north wing at Providence while Teddy and Margaret stayed in the south wing, in one of the guest rooms.

"The land is up on St. Charles Avenue, Papa," Sarah told us one evening. "It is very high up and quite beautiful. Once the weather improves, we should all ride out to take a look. We intend to start building in the spring."

"Well, I hope you will stay at Providence until the house is ready," I said. I loved having my children around me, and I knew that Teddy and Margaret would also be with us for a while.

"Of course, Mother, if that is agreeable. Ernest is going to build us a house just as fine as Providence ... but I told him, didn't I dear, that nothing can ever compare with Providence?"

Ernest smiled. "I will try and make Hamilton House as delightful for you, my love, as the home in which you grew up," he replied.

"Hamilton House! What an excellent name," said Gideon. "I like it already."

So, on a sunny, mild morning in early February, we all drove up in carriages to the Rockland area to inspect Ernest and Sarah's acreage. Knowing her delicate condition, which she had still not announced to everyone, I was somewhat alarmed to watch her jumping from rock to rock as she pointed out features of the landscape to us all.

"The house will be built right here," she said, extending her arms in all directions. "Isn't this the most beautiful location, near to town, with high, splendid views and such good fresh air. Oh, and the soil is very good here, so rich and moist. And there are some splendid oak trees and plenty of broom and scrub oak and wonderful rock formations. Just imagine how this will look in the spring, with the sun shining on buttercups and wild flowers, and with the bright green grass and the trees all budding, as well as that incredible backdrop of the sea, the mountains and the Sooke hills. Don't you all agree it's so good to be alive in such a place and on such a day?"

We all laughed at her enthusiasm and agreed wholeheartedly with her descriptions. It was indeed a beautiful location for a house, and that day, I felt more convinced than ever that Ernest was indeed making Sarah happy.

When we all arrived back at Providence and Foo served us tea in the drawing room, Sarah suddenly spoke up over the chatter.

"Ernest and I have an announcement to make," she said. "You probably all wonder why I appear to be so deliriously happy today. Well, we have just discovered that I am expecting a baby. It will come in the summer. Isn't that the most wonderful news?"

We all showed our delight by hugging her and Ernest with enthusiasm. But Sarah was a kind soul, and I could see she was concerned about possibly hurting Margaret's feelings. "Bowery, my love," she whispered kindly. "I know it will also be your turn soon, if you can ever get my silly little brother to learn how to produce a baby again!"

"Sarah!" I exclaimed in horror. "That is so inappropriate!"

"It's all right, Mother McBride," said Margaret with a smile. "I am quite used to your impossible daughter by now. And yes, Teddy and I will undoubtedly also be making you grandparents in the future. We are simply delighted for you, though, Bridey, and you, Ernest. Congratulations."

"Thank you, Bowery."

I felt a flutter of apprehension in my heart, but no one else noticed, not even Edward, who was with us that day. Gideon was simply delighted that Sarah would be making us grandparents, and no one, thank goodness, pressed her too closely for exactly when the baby was expected. She had really not begun to show, and maybe if the baby arrived in May or June, as it undoubtedly would, instead of at least July or August, when it really should, she would be able to pass it off as premature. I am sure that she and Ernest had discussed this possibility, and they did seem happy together, so I resolved not to worry about it.

I just prayed that, in view of the circumstances, whenever the baby came, it would be healthy.

*   *   *

The weeks soon slipped by, and the building of Hamilton House was well under way when the telegram from Bertie arrived in the middle of May. Teddy and Margaret were still with us and would be until August now, because their expedition to Liverpool had been delayed while plans were set up for Teddy's research project. Margaret was delighted by the delay, as she wanted to be present when Sarah's baby arrived. As my daughter began to grow larger, I was convinced the arrival of her baby would be very soon and my daughter-in-law would most certainly be present.

The telegram's arrival, however, sent us all into a spin. It simply said:

Dear Family Stop Will be arriving at Providence around May 21st with new bride Stop Antoinette Harris and I were married aboard ship by captain last night Stop Father, you would approve of seaboard wedding Stop Can't wait for you all to meet my delightful wife Stop Fondest Bertie.

"Oh my goodness!" I said, as I sat back down in alarm. "Bertie is married!"

"Has he mentioned this Antoinette woman before?" asked Gideon.

"Well my dear, Bertie hardly ever writes anything, let alone gives us details of his love life," I said.

Sarah was smiling. "It's so typical of him. He loves to surprise us. But oh, how sad, we will be deprived of another wedding. I do hope she is nice."

Teddy interrupted. "You never know with Bertie. He always had a rather doubtful taste in women."

"Whatever do you mean, Teddy?" I asked.

"Well, Mother, his women were always rather ... what is the word I'm looking for?"

"Vulgar? Unrefined?" offered Sarah. "And some were positively coarse."

"Oh my goodness!" I repeated. "I do hope that this Antoinette is suitable."

Gideon patted my hand. "Well, I'm sure if Bertie has married her, she must be charming. Let's give him the benefit of the doubt and not pass judgment until we meet her."

"I wonder where he met her?" asked Margaret.

"Well, when he wrote before my wedding he was in Paris, and he mentioned having a surprise for us. Maybe he knew her there," offered Sarah.

"Her name is French," I added.

"Yes, but not the surname. Harris. Do we know anybody called Harris?" asked Teddy.

No one could think of anyone.

We continued to speculate over breakfast that morning, but nothing could prepare us for the reality of Antoinette Harris McBride when she arrived with my son ten days later.

CHAPTER 23

The carriage drove up the driveway, coming to a stop at the front door. Having been warned of their arrival, we were all on the porch to greet Bertie and his new bride.

At first I did not take in her appearance, because my motherly eye was directed first and foremost toward my son, who, I was relieved to see, looked extremely well and happy, dressed in a dashing dark suit. He called out his greetings to us all as he helped Antoinette from the carriage.

To say she was unrefined was an understatement. The word vulgar, although perhaps a little harsh, certainly suited her better. She looked as though she had just stepped off the stage, dressed as she was in a bright red dress of layered flounces over a crinoline petticoat. A large, purple-feathered hat completed her flamboyant ensemble. She beamed broadly at us and said: "Well I'm just so charmed to meet yo'all, and what an absolutely darlin' house!"

Gideon was the first to step forward and shake his son's hand. "Welcome home, son," he said. "And welcome, Antoinette. We are delighted to meet you ... even though somewhat surprised by Bertie's sudden news."

"Yes," I added, as I hugged Bertie. "You are very bad, son, because you gave us no warning that you were planning to marry." I extended my hand to his bride, who returned a somewhat feeble handshake.

"It was my fault, Captain and Mrs. McBride," she whimpered. "We met just a few months ago in Paris and Bertie was ... well ... honey ... what is the word? *Smitten* with me? He wanted to marry me immediately, of course, but I said we should return to his home first and get his family's approval, because this is where we would be living when Bertie takes over his father's company, right? So we set sail for

Canada this spring, but I must admit I was simply swept up by the romance of a seaboard wedding and I was terribly naughty and allowed Bertie to persuade me to marry him aboard ship. It was incredibly romantic, as you can imagine, Captain McBride."

And on and on she prattled, barely allowing anyone else to say anything. I tried to place her accent and decided she must be American from the South. Sarah finally managed to interrupt her endless chatter.

"I'm Bertie's sister, Sarah," she said. "And this is my husband, Ernest, and Bertie's twin, Teddy, and Teddy's wife, Margaret."

"Charmed, I'm sure. Oh, and Sarah you are *so* pregnant. How very delightful. You must be due *very* soon."

Sarah made a face at her father behind Antoinette's back. "Well, with surprises like Bertie has given us, it is more than likely my baby will be born at any moment!"

We all laughed at that as we headed inside, most little realizing the truth of Sarah's words. We were too busy listening to Antoinette's constant drawl as she resumed her prattle, exclaiming at everything she saw inside Providence.

"Don't you just love her, Mother?" Bertie whispered in my ear at one point.

"Em ... yes, she is quite something ...." I could honestly think of no other way to describe her.

Within a week, Antoinette had successfully managed to alienate every member of the household. Foo was especially annoyed by her constant presence in his kitchen. It was not that she wanted to take over any cooking assignment; it was simply the fact that she always found it necessary to report to him all her likes and dislikes and how she wanted certain food prepared.

She also liked to tell Lum how he should be taking care of the grounds and what he should or should not be doing when planting flowers or shrubs. And Dulcie and Beaulah were both alarmed and upset when Antoinette insisted on monopolizing their time to help her decide on an outfit, fix her hair or help her ply her face with copious makeup. And I particularly hated her condescending attitude toward Dulcie because of her colour.

One night, Bertie approached me on the subject of hiring another maid solely for Antoinette.

"That might be a good idea, Bertie, but you should pay the maid's wages."

Bertie looked at me aghast when I said that the subject was not up for further discussion.

I was already beginning to see why Antoinette might have found it attractive to marry into the McBride family, and she made this even more obvious when I met her on the stairs one morning. She was gazing at my portrait.

"Ah, Mother McBride," she said. "I was just saying to Bertie yesterday that he and I should have our portraits painted soon, just as you and the Captain did. After all, when Bertie fully takes over the company, he will be the head of McBride Transportation and, as such, we will be the owners of Providence and therefore should be depicted as such, don't you agree?"

"No, my dear Antoinette, I do not!" I replied as calmly as I could, even though my blood was boiling and I was positively seething inside. "My husband and I are far from dead and, for your information, *we* will *always* be the owners of Providence!"

And with that I swept past her on the staircase. Although I did not see her reaction, I felt sure her mouth was wide open. For once, I had actually managed to render her speechless.

Antoinette's overbearing manner offended the volatile Angelina more than anyone. Although officially retired and living in her cottage, Angelina came to me with her complaints about this woman, whom she described as "that brazen hussy your son has married!"

"She comes to my cottage all the time, Mrs. McBride. She tells me how to do things. I cannot put up with her much longer! Yesterday, she even suggested that I should move somewhere else and the cottage should be rented to someone!"

I was astounded and told Angelina not to worry. "You will always have the cottage, Angelina," I said. "We do *not* intend to move you out and rent it to someone else."

And even placid, easy-going Margaret was disturbed by her new sister-in-law. "She is quite impossible," she whispered to me one day. "How could Bertie have possibly married such a creature?' We all wanted to know the answer to that.

But it was Sarah who reacted the most strongly, by going into labour just six days after Antoinette's arrival at Providence. The fact that Bertie's new wife had upset the peaceful running of our house was, in many ways, the perfect reason for what most of the family assumed to be a premature birth. Sarah and Ernest allowed everyone to believe the baby was at least seven weeks early.

Their son, however, who was born in the south wing of Providence and came into the world with a healthy bellow from his tiny lungs, weighed in at a very respectable seven pounds. He certainly did not have the appearance of a premature baby, but his May 28th birth date was not challenged. We were all simply thrilled by his safe arrival. I was especially relieved to have Dr. Ralph confirm that he was perfectly healthy in all respects. After Sarah's long and painful labour was over, we all went in one or two at a time to inspect the latest addition to the McBride family and to congratulate Sarah and Ernest.

"He is so beautiful, isn't he, Mother?" she said to me when we were finally alone. The baby's dark eyes and mop of black hair reminded me so much of Etienne Dupont, but Ernest also had dark curly hair, so it was easy to assume he was Ernest's son. He must have inherited his dark hair from his grandmother, Fleure.

I agreed wholeheartedly with her that my little grandson was indeed the most beautiful of babies. And Gideon acted as the typical doting grandfather.

Later that evening, Sarah and Ernest announced that their new son would be called Stephen Ernest. I was the only member of the family who realised the irony behind the name Sarah had chosen for her son.

Undoubtedly the choice had been hers, for I knew that the English version of Etienne was Stephen. I sincerely hoped that Edward, who, like me, had known of her love for Etienne Dupont, would never connect the two or, if he did, would not confront me about it. I wanted the past to be over and done with, and now that our beloved grandson had arrived safely and was in good health, I sincerely hoped that would be the case.

CHAPTER 24

The weeks slipped by quickly that summer as Hamilton House began to take shape. Sarah and Ernest hoped to be in residence before Christmas.

Meanwhile, Joe and Emily Caldwell had purchased land alongside my daughter and son-in-law and were also building a home on St. Charles Avenue, and, on July 21, Emily gave birth to a beautiful healthy girl they named Letitia Anne. Our two families rejoiced once again.

One week later, Anna Caldwell married Captain Robert Falconbridge of the Royal Navy, and James and Eliza had to part with their beloved only daughter when Robert's ship set sail in August for the China Seas. After that, the happy couple would in all likelihood settle in England until Robert had another posting to North America.

The saddest part of the summer for Gideon and me was the departure of Teddy and Margaret in August. They would be travelling by train to Montreal, and from there by ship to Liverpool, where Teddy was to work on setting up his research project in Gambia. It was something he desperately wanted to do before settling down into practice.

"After two years in Africa, I intend to return to Victoria, Mother," he assured me. "Dr. Ralph wants to retire and is hoping I will take over his general practice then."

"How wonderful! I shall count the days until you return."

"But this research is important to me, Mother. I really want to make a difference in the world, and I am so lucky that Margaret has promised to come with me. She is so brave."

"Indeed she is," I said. "I pray the climate will not be too hard for her to take. And I am so proud of you, son. *Doctor* McBride," I added with a smile.

"We intend to delay having a family until we are settled back in Canada. It seems only wise, unless of course nature decides otherwise. But meanwhile, it will be a wonderful adventure and we will write constantly, telling you everything."

They finally left, amidst tears from us all. We bade them a fond farewell and safe journey to England and Africa. The house seemed very quiet after they left, save for the constant prattle of Antoinette, who appeared more and more dissatisfied with her married life. Bertie was working hard alongside Gideon every day, learning to take over the day-to-day running of the company. He was enjoying the work enormously and was proving to be a first-rate businessman to follow in his father's footsteps. However, his constant attention to business left his new bride with time on her hands.

Gideon suggested that perhaps Bertie should buy their own home, and that being mistress of her own domain would give Antoinette something positive to do. I thought this was an excellent idea, as she was beginning to irritate me beyond belief. There were many houses in James Bay, some quite grand, that would suit them well. Bertie also thought it an admirable idea, but Antoinette was still entertaining the thought of one day being the chatelaine of Providence. I vowed inwardly that that was never going to happen if I could help it.

And so the year 1897 gradually grew to a close. Sarah, Ernest and little Stephen moved into Hamilton House in early November and were joined one month later by their neighbours, Joe, Emily and baby Letitia Caldwell. Bertie had managed to persuade the impossible Antoinette to look at some houses in James Bay, and finally they had decided on one that seemed to suit them both. Antoinette then set about spending Bertie's money recklessly on furnishings and staff to help her run the establishment.

Christmas was somewhat quieter that year. It was just Gideon and me, Sarah, Ernest and Stephen, and Bertie and Antoinette. But we all enjoyed spoiling little Stephen on his first Christmas.

Edward spent Christmas Day with James and Eliza at Joe and Emily's house, cooing over their little Letty. They were all missing Anna and Robert, and now even Kit had departed the family nest. In late November, he had taken off for the Klondike, where there was talk of a new gold rush. Unlike his brother Joe, father James and grandfather Edward, he had no interest in becoming a lawyer. He wanted to be his own man and was determined to find new opportunities in the north, where many others from Victoria were heading with similar ideas.

I could see the gleam of excitement about that news of gold in Gideon and Edward's eyes, and I wondered if men ever truly grow out of holding impossible dreams for a life of adventure inspired by the magic of gold.

On Boxing Day, the McBrides and the Caldwells joined for dinner at Hamilton House, and I expressed my views about the foolishness of men who constantly go in search of gold at the end of the rainbow. I was immediately decried by both families.

"My dear wife," said Gideon with a grin. "Had Edward and I not come north on a whim to seek our fortunes in 1858, I would never have met you and we would not all be enjoying the fruits of those labours today."

"Most of the fruits we enjoy, Gideon, have come about from your hard work—not by the gold you retrieved in the goldfields."

"Goodness me," interrupted Antoinette. "Did you gentlemen actually find gold in the Cariboo? Or was it all humbug, as so many people said?"

Gideon and Edward's eyes gleamed with amusement as Gideon replied, "Oh yes, indeed, Antoinette, we found nuggets the size of large pumpkins! The gold was there, lying on the ground, just for the picking."

"Oh my goodness! You must indeed have made a fortune."

"They are teasing you, Antoinette," I said, although I was rather enjoying her astonishment also. On the other hand, I could see her brain ticking, working out just how much her father-in-law must be worth, and I did not want her to get even more ideas of how she could spend Bertie's money.

She then began asking questions about the news from the Klondike. "It must be *so* exciting to arrive in a new town when there is a gold rush on," she sighed. "Just imagine how very rich you could become." She had a faraway look in her eyes. I glanced at Bertie and saw he was somewhat irritated by her remarks.

Times were indeed changing. Our children and their children were growing older. It was the natural progression of life, but, for the first time that Christmas I began to realize how fleeting our time on earth really is. I wanted things to slow down, even though I knew that could not possibly happen.

CHAPTER 25

The year 1898 was full of poignant highs and dreadful lows.

In February, the new Legislative Building was finally completed and looked very grand, sitting majestically across the James Bay mudflats. The McBrides and the Caldwells all attended the opening ceremonies *en masse* to support Edward. who was still embroiled in politics as a member of the legislature for Esquimalt. He had frequently threatened to retire from politics and the law but seemed to enjoy both far too much to leave either.

The first meeting of the legislature occurred on February 10, and old Bishop Cridge, who stated that he could easily remember the very first meeting of the legislature back in 1860, in the old buildings dubbed "the bird cages," took part in all the ceremonies, along with other MLAs like Edward and Dr. Helmcken, who had been the first Speaker of the House. It was a moving ceremony, and Gideon and I, now considered valued pioneers in Victoria, felt very much a part of history that day.

But there were also rumblings of war around the world, the first being the Spanish-American war and later the unrest in South Africa with the Boers, who were Dutch settlers in that part of Africa. This particularly concerned me, knowing that Teddy and Margaret had now arrived in Senegambia in Africa. Teddy was part of a team carrying out an expeditionary investigation into the first trypanosome to be found in human blood.

I didn't understand all the implications of this important research work, other than the fact that it was connected to an insect known as the tsetse fly, which carried the disease, but I was extremely proud of Teddy, who assured me in his many letters that they were perfectly safe and were far from where the trouble with the Boers was brewing.

Gambia was a British colony and protectorate on the West African bulge, a long, narrow strip of land running from the mouth of the River Gambia. It was surrounded by the French colony of Senegambia, so Teddy's knowledge of French had proved most useful. I studied the area in my atlas, and Gideon and I religiously followed our son's progress with every letter he wrote.

Those letters were in fact my salvation during 1898 and 1899, because Gideon once again began to suffer symptoms of his old medical problem. The cancer in his stomach, which had been in remission for some years, was again causing him trouble, and there was little that Dr. Ralph could prescribe that would help the pain and discomfort. Gideon was a strong man, however, and he fought a gallant fight, often not allowing me to see his pain. But I could sense the agony he was experiencing and I witnessed the pain in his eyes that on many occasions he found impossible to hide. He also began to lose weight in an alarming manner.

I found myself constantly on the alert, watching my husband for the first signs of pain, wishing desperately I could erase his distress, and wondering how I would ever survive should something happen to him.

Gideon loved me to read Teddy's letters to him. Sometimes we sat together up in the turret reading them. On other occasions, we enjoyed the sun's warmth on the veranda. When I look back on those times of peace and harmony between us, of complete and utter understanding and love, I realized how fortunate I was to have Gideon in my life those many years. I had come so far from the miseries of Field House and the trials of being in service. He had helped me to overcome and survive my past, and it was almost as though I had lived two separate lives and been two completely different people.

Gideon had enabled me to become Jane McBride, proud wife and mother, living in such pleasant, luxurious surroundings in a country I had grown to love as much as he did. I was indeed a very lucky woman.

In many ways, those months were made even more enjoyable by the presence of both Bertie and Sarah, who seemed to be constantly dropping by to visit us at Providence, and we did not object. Although nothing was ever said, I believe our children both sensed in their own way that their father's life was nearing its end. Sarah often brought little Stephen to Providence with her, and Gideon played with him and told him stories of the sea, just as he had done with Sarah, Teddy and Bertie.

Bertie came often, thankfully without Antoinette most of the time, as though he understood how much she irritated us both. And on those occasions, he talked with his father about the future plans of McBride Transportation.

"We have expanded in the past, father, but now I think the time has come to diversify," he said one day.

"How do you mean, son? I'm always open to new ideas."

"What would you think about us purchasing some canneries on the Fraser?"

Gideon thought for a moment and a smile crept over his face. "You must have been reading the same material I have," he replied. "Salmon canning! It seems to be a great opportunity, I agree."

"I have indeed read a great deal about it, and there are currently two canneries for sale," Bertie continued. "We should get in at the bottom and learn all that there is to know. Salmon canning seems to have a very lucrative future ahead of it."

"I agree ... albeit reluctantly ... because I vowed long ago I would never have anything more to do with fish!" He laughed. "Anyway, Bertie, bring me all the details and we'll look into purchasing those canneries."

I knew it made Gideon feel good to have something new and exciting to think about, and I was happy for him.

The constant stream of letters from Teddy and Margaret also brought us joy and brought them closer to us. Teddy's descriptive prose of life in Africa, and dear Margaret's sweet personal notes, made us all feel we, too, were experiencing their adventures.

Dearest Mother and Father:

We left Liverpool taking with us all manner of equipment. I am sharing the responsibilities of this project with a chap called Harvey Winslow. He is great fun, and Margaret likes him too. I insist that she stays in town when Harvey and I go off into the bush, but you know how stubborn my dear wife can be. I know she will want to assist us as much as possible—and she is very useful on the administration side, keeping our notes in order etc.

Our instruments and laboratory equipment take up an awful lot of room. We are of course also taking a mosquito-proof tent which we can erect in whatever native town we happen to find ourselves. We hope to observe them swarming like bees around the top of a closed jam pot ....

Once they had settled in Gambia, Teddy's next letter said:

We have three cameras with us and an old gramophone. The gram-ophone amuses the natives while we gain their confidence in us allowing their blood to be examined.

... oh dear parents and family, the sights we have seen are incredible! The African landscape and the wildlife! I cannot begin to describe such beauty. This morning I saw a pure white heron. The colours of some of the birds are very exotic indeed—a kingfisher with beak and legs of bright red; a little scarlet and black finch ... such incredible colours ...

But later, there were also letters where Teddy described in vivid detail the suffering he encountered and the desperate need for work such as theirs. Gambia was at the very centre of much tropical disease, and Teddy frequently told us how glad he was to have the opportunity to make a difference and be on the brink of possibly some new discovery to save mankind.

There was a long gap between his letters in early 1899, and when one finally came it was to tell us that poor Margaret had experienced two bouts of malaria. She was now recovered, but he worried constantly about her and insisted she always stay in town while he and Harvey went out in the field.

After all, we are just a couple of fool doctors, but Margaret is far more precious.

We have no books to guide us, but we know already a good deal more concerning these beastly parasites. We know, for instance, that our particular parasite is a very important one and is probably responsible for a good many of the deaths we encounter on a daily basis. Our progress reports are being reported throughout Africa, so our little beast is becoming very famous.

I have to tell you something very amusing that happened while on a mission. We encountered a fellow who enquired if I wanted to purchase one of his wives! He has seven apparently and finds them rather too much for him! I told him that I had a perfectly lovely wife and wanted no other, and then told him he was a bad "mahometan," since he had seven wives instead of the accepted four. He also drank whisky and ate pig (both forbidden) and was therefore sure to go to yahaniba (hell). After that he promptly left me alone!

Margaret plays her little music box, and the natives love its tinkling sound. They are also intrigued by my gold teeth and think I must be very rich.

In our dispensary in town, we see numerous cases covering various ailments, some minor such as coughs and colds, but we did encounter one interesting case of elephantiasis and anaemia.

We have also discovered a wonderful and important drug of a new variety which is very effective in heart disease. Further inland, the natives had been using this potion for poison on their arrows! Oh, father, how I wish I could discover something which would cure your beastly C ailment.

In late June of 1899, when Gideon's condition seemed to be worsening, another letter arrived from Teddy and Margaret which gladdened our hearts.

"You will be pleased to know that we will be returning to Canada before the end of the year. The climate is bad for Margaret and, by then, I will have completed almost two years of research and will be glad to settle down to private practice in Victoria.

I am so glad that I came however. It has been a wonderful experience, even though we have really done nothing very wonderful so far. We have only proved that there is far more tsetse fly disease on this coast and in Central Africa than was ever suspected and that it does occur in human beings, and must be reckoned with in diagnosing chronic tropical illnesses.

We will be back in Liverpool by late September, and in Victoria hopefully before Christmas. So looking forward to seeing you all again ...

Teddy was indeed being modest by saying he had done nothing very wonderful in Africa. We were delighted to hear of the praise he received both in England and Canada on his return, and when he was awarded the prestigious Order of Leopold for his work from the very grateful Belgian king, our hearts were bursting with pride.

There was a certain irony in the fact that this news reached us when it did, because Gideon's condition gradually began to grow worse, and I feared that Teddy would not arrive in time to see his father before the end. Oh, how easy it was to write about the inevitable, but I could not, and would not, accept it. Not yet. I knew miracles could happen.

They must, for I could not bear life without Gideon.

CHAPTER 26

On Saturday, November 25, 1899, Teddy and Margaret arrived home. It was so good to see them both, and Gideon rallied to the occasion as best he could.

Margaret's complexion was sallow and she looked very thin, but Teddy insisted she would soon be better, once in the more pleasant climate of Canada. They both sat with Gideon and talked of their adventures until he grew tired, and then we allowed him to sleep.

Teddy also talked to Dr. Ralph about his father's condition, but both doctors realized there was very little that could be done to save him. Gideon was now being prescribed heavy doses of morphine to alleviate the pain, and by the following Tuesday he was confined to his bed all day, being too weak to stand.

On Wednesday morning he called for both his sons and requested that they carry him up to the turret. Foo was asked to erect a cot up there for him by the window, and my armchair was placed beside it. For the next three days, I slept in the chair with a blanket covering me, and my hand in his. Most of the time he slept, but occasionally he came out of his semi-coma and asked me a question or simply smiled at me. His beautiful eyes that had looked at me so often with passion, took on a dreamy, faraway look whenever he turned his head towards the window and gazed out at the harbour and the distant mountains.

"What adventures we have had, my love," he said.

"We will have more, Gideon."

He closed his eyes and slept peacefully for a while.

He had so many visitors— Sarah, Ernest, little Stephen, Teddy and Margaret, Bertie and, on one occasion, Antoinette. When I heard her voice coming from our bedroom below, I stood up, walked down the stairs and confronted her as calmly as I was able.

"Antoinette, would you mind repeating what you just said?" I asked.

"Why, dear Mother McBride, I simply said that I find a house of mourning so depressing," she said.

"Bertie." I turned to my son. "Would you kindly tell your wife that this is *not* a house of mourning. Your father is still alive, and if she finds coming here so depressing for her, please remove her from my house. I do not wish to look at her right now."

With that I turned my back and headed back up to the turret.

"Well, really!" I heard her say. "Whatever is the matter with her? I was just stating the obvious, honey."

"I think it best if I take you home, Antoinette," replied Bertie. "You've said more than enough. I will visit Father alone in future. I do not wish Mother to be upset any more than she already is."

I heard their voices retreat into the distance. She was still complaining, and my son was defending me. I was so proud of him, and I was glad she was gone.

Edward came later, and he sat talking quietly with his old friend, reminiscing about the past. Then Skiff came up with Dulcie, and I saw tears trickling down Skiff's cheeks when he left the room. None of us could bear to see what had happened to Gideon, once so strong and large as life itself; now just a shrunken, emaciated shadow of his former self.

But to me, he was still my beloved husband. I held his hand, willing my strength into his body, praying for the miracle I knew might never happen.

Late on Friday night of December 1, he woke suddenly from a coma-induced sleep and squeezed my hand more tightly than usual. I had been dozing but was immediately alert again.

"Gideon, what is it?"

"Jane, my love. Why don't you sleep in our bed downstairs? You will be more comfortable there."

"I won't leave you, Gideon."

"But ... you must. We have to ... part now, my love. You have to let me ... go."

"No! No! Don't say that. Don't say that. Not yet. I cannot ... I cannot ..."

"You are strong, little Jane."

"Not without you."

"Yes ... yes ... always strong. So small and ... yet ... so strong ... It was so easy to fall in love with you."

He lifted his other hand to touch my cheek and then reached for the leather strap around his neck which held the circular piece of metal his mother had given him so long ago. "Take ... take it off me, Jane. Place it ... round your neck now. It will keep you safe always, and one day it will ... it will bring you home again to me."

"Oh Gideon ... no ... please, please don't leave me."

"Yes, I ... must." His voice was suddenly stronger and for one brief moment I thought he was recovering. The miracle had happened. His eyes were no longer blurry but were bright as they looked into mine. "Do this for me, my love. You *must* do it. This time you must face death because you ... are ... you are a brave woman, Jane."

"I can't, Gideon. I can't ..." I whispered, even as my hands were removing the talisman and placing it around my own neck. "I cannot live without you."

"Yes, you will be strong. Remember little Caleb. I will see him again soon ... but please, Jane, don't be as you were then. Remember, life must go on for those who are left. You did it then and you can do it again ..."

His breath was laboured and his voice was fading again, and I could see his strength was leaving his pain-wracked body.

I knew instinctively what he was trying to tell me. I must not bury my hurt, as I had done when my small son had died all those years ago. This time I must grieve openly and face my loss. I must be strong. *But how?*

I smiled at him through my tears. "I will be strong, Gideon. I promise.

"For Sarah and the boys, too. It will be hard for them ... they will be sad ... especially my little Sweetpea ..."

"I know. And Edward and James and all the Caldwells."

"They ... they will take care of you, little one. Gather them around you."

His eyes closed and he was sleeping again. Once during the night he awoke and whispered my name. "Jane, Jane."

"I'm here, my love."

"I ... love ... you ..."

They were his final words. When he closed his eyes again, it was for the last time. From afar, I heard my voice calmly calling for the family, who had all been staying at Providence that night. And, one by one, they came in to say their farewells.

That night and over the coming days, weeks and months, I was so consumed with my own grief that I was barely aware of what was happening around me.

I do know that there were hundreds of people at Gideon's funeral. His employees from all over British Columbia, his business acquaintances, his friends and, of course, our immediate and extended family. People came up to me afterwards expressing their sorrow, gripping my hand, whispering their words of comfort, but afterwards I did not remember their faces or their names. I walked as though in a trance, recalling simply that it was a long stream of people who spoke to me. But, over time, everything became blurred and hazy.

After the funeral I simply wanted to be alone. I retreated into the depths of my despair and barely spoke to anyone. I knew I was breaking my promise to Gideon, but I told myself that when things got better, I would come back to the world again. *But would things ever get better?*

Providence was my haven. I had no wish to leave the house, other than to take the occasional walk up to St. Luke's and sit by Gideon's grave, beside that of little Caleb in the McBride family plot.

One day I shall be there too, I told myself. I prayed that God would make it soon, because life without Gideon was unbearable.

I knew my family needed me. Sarah was devastated by her father's death, but I could not open my arms or my heart to her. I reasoned that she had Ernest to comfort her. And Teddy had Margaret, who was a tower of strength for us all in the weeks that followed. She gladly took over running Providence on my behalf.

Bertie spent more and more time at Providence. I never asked him about Antoinette. I sensed that not only was he struggling to deal with his father's death and taking over complete responsibility for the company, but also his marriage was in bad trouble. He probably needed me to talk with, but somehow I was unable to help him, either.

Even dear Edward stopped visiting Providence after a while, perhaps sensing the black cloud that was hanging over the house. In his own despair at losing his friend, he found it difficult to comfort me, especially when I made it obvious that I did not want to be comforted.

One of the many visitors who came to Providence to offer me condolences was a man by the name of William Baron. I did not remember him at first, until he reintroduced himself as Willow, the young native boy who had attended school with Sarah and the boys.

He was now a tall, handsome man dressed like a gentleman. I found it hard to connect the two images I had of him, one the barefoot, ragamuffin native boy in his canoe, and the other this well-spoken, polished, well-educated man.

"You know, of course, Mrs. McBride, that your late husband was instrumental in helping me gain a first-class education. I will never forget his generosity," he said.

"He assisted many young people, Mr. Baron. I am glad he was able to help you with your dream of becoming a lawyer."

"I was deeply saddened by the news of his death and am only sorry I was not able to be here in time for his funeral. I live and work in Toronto now but hope one day to return to Victoria and help some of my people here. The laws are changing slowly."

"They are indeed. And I appreciate you calling on me."

He paused for a moment before continuing. "I hear that your daughter is married to Mr. Ernest Hamilton."

"Yes," I replied, although I did not want our discussion to continue. I wanted to be alone.

"Is she happy in the marriage?"

What an extraordinary question, I thought. *What business is that of his?*

"Of course, Mr. Baron, but naturally the death of her beloved father has been an enormous blow to her."

"Of course ... well, I will leave you now, Mrs. McBride. Thank you again for seeing me, and please accept my sincere condolences at your loss."

He bowed over my hand and suddenly, for no apparent reason, a shiver ran down my spine. I had felt a sudden dislike for him and his overbearing, sugary words. I could not decide if they were sincere or not.

PART THREE

Looking Ahead

JANE
(1900-1906)

CHAPTER 27

JANE

I still think of the year 1900 as being a particularly grim one for all the McBrides. We were all fighting our own particular demons following Gideon's death at the end of 1899, and none of us seemed capable of sharing our troubles and grief with the others. If we had, we might well have averted further pain.

Margaret succumbed to another bout of malaria early in the new year, which once again left her weak and completely drained. Teddy took such good care of her, pampering her as a loving husband should, but emotionally Margaret was a strong woman, even if she were not physically strong. I admired her courage.

In the late spring of 1900, Bertie announced that he was selling his house in James Bay and he and Antoinette were separating. I was not surprised to hear this and almost welcomed his news.

"I will have the distinction of being the first divorced member of the McBride clan, Mother," he told me wryly.

"Oh Bertie, I'm so sorry ... but she never seemed right for you, dear."

"I realize that now. I was just besotted with her initially. Goodness only knows why. I sensed from the beginning she was only interested in me because of my money and my connections back here. When I met her in Paris, she was with her parents, who I later learned had lost a fortune and were completely impoverished. They were displaying their daughter around Paris in order to catch an unsuspecting man with money. I became the target."

"Oh Bertie ..." was all I could offer. We had all sensed the truth long ago, but finally Bertie himself had seen it also.

"She has also been constantly unfaithful to me during our marriage, Mother, with any number of men."

"Good heavens!" This really did shock me.

"And she has now found one with money who is going to whisk her away to Australia, where apparently he owns a sheep ranch and numerous acres of land and is very wealthy. Oh, and incidentally, she tells me she is pregnant."

"Oh no! But Bertie, is it ... your child?"

"No chance, Mother. She is reluctant to admit when the child is due, but in any event we have not ... had ... relations for quite a while. I presume the father is the Australian chap."

I was embarrassed to be discussing such personal things with my son, but I pursued the conversation a little further. "But Bertie, should you not be absolutely sure before you allow her to go? She might after all be carrying *your* child."

"I doubt it, and in any event, it is best she leave. I am not cut out to be a husband and probably not a father either. I make a much better bachelor!"

"You are welcome to move back into the south wing at Providence, dear," I said.

"I was hoping you would suggest I move back in, Mother."

I had enjoyed having Teddy and Margaret home again in the north wing and had not pushed them to move out to their own place because Teddy was now working long hours as a doctor, having taken over Dr. Ralph's practice, which left Margaret on her own a good deal. She never complained and seemed to enjoy staying with me, even though I was not particularly good company. On Teddy's part, he was simply relieved that his wife was not completely alone while she recovered from her bout of malaria.

And so we had turned the century and somehow managed to survive all our inner turmoil. There were also many changes in the city. I had lived now in Victoria for almost forty years, and most had been happy, save for the months since Gideon passed away. But I feared for the young people of today. The war was lingering in Africa, and what, I wondered, would lie ahead?

And then, early in the year 1901, our beloved Queen Victoria passed away at Osborne House in England, leaving her empire in a state of turmoil. Her namesake city was again thrust into mourning.

CHAPTER 28

The Queen's heir, the notorious Prince of Wales, had spent a lifetime waiting in the wings to take over the role of sovereign, and many of us now wondered and fretted about how this elderly reprobate would handle his prestigious position. It seemed, however, that the empire need not have worried, because initially the new king appeared to handle the great honour bestowed upon him with dignity. But he was certainly not anything like his mother and would apparently take the throne with new ideas and a mind of his own. His coronation was planned for the following June.

In Victoria we followed the developments with interest, but England was far away and there was more to occupy our thoughts nearer home. Our telephone service was extended throughout the city and into Saanichton and Sidney on the peninsula, and by the fall we could even make telephone calls to as far away as Duncan and Nanaimo, up island.

The Boers were finally being defeated in Africa, and our world was growing smaller by means of easier, quicker communication methods.

On one particularly warm spring morning in 1902, I decided it was high time for me to go out and face the world. I decided to visit Sarah at Hamilton House and see my little grandson, who was now almost five years old. I often wondered why Sarah had not presented him with a brother or sister by now, but I never asked her, and she had not volunteered any information on the subject.

I called Lum for the horse and carriage and decided to drive myself over to Sarah's. The road to Rockland was an easy route, and I felt I was quite able to handle it. Heading out of town, I admired the new spring blooms and cherry blossoms along the way. For the first time in a long while, I began to enjoy my surroundings and feel a sort of peace growing within me. That morning as I was dressing, I had distinctly heard Gideon's voice talking to me, telling me I had better hurry up and get on with life. I had a strong feeling he was around me somewhere that morning.

As I drove up the driveway to Hamilton House, I again admired the tall white pillars and elegance of the home that Ernest had built for my daughter. Then I noticed another carriage pulled up by the front door. I hesitated for a moment, assuming they had company, and I did not want to intrude. I began to wish I had telephoned Sarah first.

However, it was too late now, so I drew the carriage to a stop behind the other one, which I did not recognize. I alighted and decided I might go around the side of the house first, in case they were sitting on the patio, this being such a beautiful, warm day. I was anxious to see little Stephen and felt he would probably be playing on the lawn.

Much to my surprise, there was no one around, but the French doors were wide open, so I climbed the steps to the patio and entered the house that way, calling to Sarah as I came into the sun room. There was no reply—just an eerie silence. It was particularly unusual not to hear Stephen's voice, playing with his toys. I called again as I headed through the drawing room and out into the hall. It was so strange to find no one, not even a servant, around.

And then I heard voices. One was Sarah's. The other I did not recognize immediately, but they were coming from upstairs.

"Sarah, are you home?" I called again.

I heard what I thought was her whispering, "Stay there, it's my mother."

And then she descended the stairs, in the process of covering herself in a wrap. "Oh Mother, I'm sorry, I was taking a nap."

"In mid-morning?"

"Yes! I was ... not feeling well. How did you get in?"

"The French doors were wide open. I thought you had company ... seeing the carriage outside?"

"Oh ... that! Yes, someone left it here last night. We had guests for dinner."

"Really?"

"Mother, why are you so suspicious?"

"Where is my grandson? And Ernest?"

"Nanny took Stephen for a walk. And Ernest is working all day. The other servants have the day off, so I went back to bed as I have a terrific headache."

"Well, I'm sorry to disturb you, but I thought I heard voices."

"You were mistaken." She was now facing me in the hall, and I knew she was not about to invite me to stay for tea or a visit, so I made to turn. But at that moment I caught a glimpse of two feet on the top landing, attempting to hide behind a potted plant.

"Perhaps I was *not* mistaken, Sarah. Tell your *guest* to join us ..."

"I was about to come down anyway, Mrs. McBride. Sarah, there is no point in lying to your mother anymore." It was William Baron, also in a state of half undress, but tactfully trying to button his shirt as he descended the stairs.

"Mr. Baron! May I ask exactly what you were doing upstairs in my daughter's home when she is here alone?"

He smiled. "Exactly! Oh, Mrs. McBride, I think not. You see, I am the soul of discretion. It would not be appropriate for me to describe *exactly* what we were doing, but I am sure your imagination can ..."

"Stop it, Willow," shouted Sarah. "Stop it immediately."

I turned to face Willow, or William Baron or whatever he called himself now, and suddenly I was extremely angry. I realized then why I had not liked him before. But I was even more angry with my daughter, and I intended to tell her so.

"Mr. Baron, will you please leave right now. I wish to speak with my daughter alone."

"Sarah, do you wish me to go?" He raised an eyebrow at her.

"Yes, you had better leave, Willow, please," she replied.

He then had the audacity to bend down and kiss her on the lips right in front of me before walking to the door. "Ladies, I bid you farewell," he said with a bow, "And I will contact you later, Sarah."

She did not reply. He was gone and we were alone.

"All right, Mother. Say what you have to say. I know you are anxious to tell me what a wicked woman I am, so go ahead. You won't be telling me anything I don't already know."

"Oh, I think I will! Firstly, Sarah, you obviously have no morals. Secondly, I cannot imagine how you could do such a thing to Ernest, the best and most honourable of men. A man, I might add, who took you in marriage knowing you were pregnant with another's man child. He has been the kindest of husbands, giving you everything you desire ... and this, *this* is how you repay him! I am disgusted. I cannot believe you are my daughter."

"No, I am sure you can't, Mother. I have never measured up to your precious standards anyway. You are absolutely right. I have no morals. I am wicked. I am evil. Ernest *is* a dear, sweet, kind man and has been the best husband possible, but I have always craved something more. I cannot explain it and I don't know how or why ... it is just the way I am. And then Willow came back into my life and I tried—believe me, I tried so hard to resist him, but it reminded me—the feelings reminded me of how I had once felt about Etienne. The passion I had longed for." She paused before adding in a small, desperate voice, "Oh, Mother, I know it was wrong."

"Wrong? Wrong?" I screamed back at her. "Just you listen to me, young lady, and listen well. It was much more than wrong. It was deceitful and wicked. You have a husband and a child to think about. And here you are, in the middle of the day, in broad daylight, carrying on an illicit affair with someone else. I presume you sent all the servants away, but anyone could have walked through the patio doors, just as I did. Anyone! Even Ernest. If you were searching for passion you should have *made* it happen with Ernest."

"I tried ... but then, after Papa died, I felt so lost and alone, and the grief was so overwhelming. I tried to talk to you about it ... but, as usual, you were distant and aloof. You have only expressed your love for one of your children, the one who died before I was born. Teddy, Bertie and I were always just substitutes for him."

Her words stunned me, but I was not about to stop my tirade now. "Oh, Sarah, that is not true. How dare you twist this and blame me because of what you have done by having an adulterous relationship with this ... this ..."

"Say it, mother! This Indian? That's what you're thinking, isn't it?"

"No, it is not. I don't care what race or religion he is. You have still committed adultery, and I am ashamed of you, Sarah."

I took her arm and forced her to come with me into the drawing room. We sat facing each other on the sofa while I tried to cool my rising temper. Suddenly I was afire with emotion once again, and I could hear Gideon's voice telling me how I should deal with this. It would be hard, but I knew I must be strong for Sarah now, so that her marriage could be saved.

"Sarah, listen to me. You will never, I repeat *never*, see that man again. And you will be a good, faithful wife to Ernest from now on ... whatever it takes ... for the sake of your sweet little boy."

"Oh, so you want to tell me how to run my life yet again, Mother?"

"I am not running your life. I am just stating a fact. Because I promise you, if you carry on this affair, I will do everything in my power to take Stephen away from you ... and, what is more, I might even tell Ernest of your infidelity."

"But that would only hurt him, and I know you wouldn't do that to him," she countered.

"You're right, Sarah. He would be hurt. It would destroy him. So, think about that. But, at the same time, remember what I have said. This adulterous affair must stop. I mean it! You have to learn *how* to make your marriage work, and be happy and content with Ernest. Stephen deserves parents who love each other."

"They did, mother. They did love each other so very much ..." I saw tears beginning to well up in her eyes.

We had come to blows so many times, my daughter and I. We would never completely agree on anything. We were so different, but I felt that morning that she understood my determination and resolve, and in many ways agreed with me. Perhaps she was glad that finally I had discovered her indiscretion and would put an end to a matter that had grown out of her control. Even my criticism of her was perhaps showing her that I really did care.

Was I to blame? I wondered. If I had tried harder to understand her, to help her, to love her, would her life have been different? Would she not have rebelled quite so much if I had been more loving?

I patted her hand then. "Now, go upstairs, Sarah, and take a long bath and get dressed before your son returns. I will wait here for him and Nanny." I paused before adding, "There are going to be some changes from now on in all our lives. I have just decided that tonight I am having a family dinner at Providence and will invite your Uncle Edward and James and Eliza. Perhaps Joe and Emily and little Letty can come too. And you and Ernest and Stephen, of course. There will also be Margaret and Teddy, if he is not working, and Bertie also. It is about time our two families were all together again. It has been far too long. Now ... off you go, because after Stephen returns and I visit with him for a while, I must hurry home and warn Foo he has a large dinner to prepare."

Sarah looked at me in amazement. "Mother, this is the first time in a long while that you have been so ..."

"Alive? Forceful?" I added. "Yes, I think your father would want this. He always told me that life must go on."

When I was alone while Sarah took her bath, I began thinking how glad I was that something had made me come to Hamilton House on that particular morning. Whatever it was had made me realize that I had to take back my life again.

Afterwards, driving home at a speedy clip in the trap, I felt alive again. During the past hour, I had experienced shock, horror, despair and rage. But once again, I was tingling with emotions, and it felt remarkably good. I was once more Jane McBride.

Yes, I had finally come back to life again, and Gideon would be proud of me.

CHAPTER 29

Everyone came to dinner that night, despite the short notice.

Dear Foo was beside himself with excitement. He always functioned best under pressure, and there was nothing he enjoyed more than presenting a first-class dinner in the dining room of Providence. As long as he had assistance with serving the meal, which he did that night with both Dulcie and Beaulah, he was completely happy. So, while Sarah's nanny supervised supper for the little ones in the nursery upstairs, the adults dined in splendour downstairs.

I think everyone was surprised to witness the change in my demeanour. I had suddenly discarded my mournful widow bearing, that I had carried around for so long, and replaced it with a stronger, firmer, more determined person. I had even dressed in a light grey rather than my usual sombre black. I sat at the head of the table and led the conversation that night, instead of remaining silent.

I brought up Gideon's name frequently and invited others to share their memories of him. Edward seemed especially relieved to be able to talk of Gideon again in my presence. We were finally honouring my husband the way we should have done many months earlier.

Bertie told us about the canning industry and all that he had managed to achieve after the purchase of the two canneries on the Fraser. The name McBride was fast becoming known in the salmon canning world now, and our label McBride's Finest was a household word.

We then talked about the upcoming coronation to be held in London in June. The Prince of Wales would be crowned King Edward VII, and the city was abuzz with the news of all the elaborate preparations underway in England.

"Although I have not spoken with you of this yet, Sarah," announced Ernest suddenly, "I thought that the two of us might take an extended trip to England and be there in time to witness all the pomp and ceremony. What do you think, my love? We could leave in May?"

"But what about Stephen?" she replied.

I immediately intervened. "He could stay with me, Sarah. I would love to have him, and then the two of you would be free to enjoy yourselves in England."

She glared at me briefly, but was immediately overridden again by Emily Caldwell, who added, "And we could share him between us. Stephen could stay with us for part of the time. Letty would adore it. They get on so well together, and we are just next door."

"There!" I said. "So it's settled. It's a wonderful idea, Ernest, and will do you both a world of good."

Sarah's expression clearly told me what she was thinking. I was taking control of her life yet again, but it had been pure coincidence that Ernest had suggested the trip just at the right time. I felt this trip would help remove all temptation for Sarah, and maybe while she and her husband were away they would get their marriage back on a firm footing. It was ideal.

"So, my love," said the ever-patient Ernest. "We will have a wonderful, worry-free excursion. I will begin making plans to leave soon."

"Oh Ernest, please let me think about it first."

"What's to think about?" I again intervened. "Go ahead, Ernest, reserve tickets on the train and ship. We will all take care of Stephen, don't worry."

"Thank you, Mother McBride," Ernest replied.

Sarah continued to stare at me in annoyance. Although she might agree that it was a good thing, she hated me to be the one to organize things for her. In her mind, this was control.

We then all began to talk about London and the many sights that Sarah and Ernest would see, and we all agreed how lucky they were to be going at such a fortuitous time.

After everyone left that night and the house was quiet again, I felt better than I had for a long time. I had a sweet daughter-in-law and son living in the house, another son who was also back in Providence without his odious, unfaithful wife, and a daughter whose marriage I hoped I had managed to save from disaster.

I allowed Beaulah to brush my hair for a long time as I sat in front of the mirror thinking, because her action was so soothing. I was envisioning the joy of soon having little Stephen staying with us and running across the lawns of Providence. Gideon and I had always wanted to fill the house with children and laughter.

Suddenly I had something to look forward to again, instead of that ghastly dark space I had only been able to see ahead of me after Gideon's death. I was thinking once again, planning, and even smiling. *Thank you, Gideon,* I whispered to the empty room.

And then another idea popped into my head. Automobiles were beginning to make the news, and one had already been seen on the streets of Victoria. I decided that maybe I would buy myself one.

I was amazed by my own daring.

CHAPTER 30

Sarah and Ernest left for their trip to England on the first day of May, and Stephen moved into the nursery with his nanny. He was a complete joy to have around, and I know Margaret, who had still not been able to conceive, was especially thrilled to have him. She spent hours reading to him, playing with him and taking him for walks. His nanny began to think her presence was hardly required.

In the middle of June, he moved over to Joe and Emily Caldwell's home in Rockland and was able to play with Letty. They were both six years old now, and very bright for their age. When news reached us that the king's coronation in London had been postponed until August due to his emergency surgery for appendicitis, Ernest and Sarah wrote that they had decided to stay on until the end of August and would sail home then. I took this as a good sign that their marriage was once more back on an even keel.

Stephen did not appear to miss his parents unduly. He enjoyed having so many people fussing around him and spent his days between the Caldwells and all of us at Providence. He and Letty became inseparable. This was especially good for Stephen, for, being an only child, he had seemed lonely. Letty, on the other hand, had two younger brothers, William and John, but she much preferred to play with Stephen.

With Edward's advice and assistance, I went ahead and purchased my automobile in July from a dealer in town by the name of Bagster, who imported the machines from San Francisco. It was a steam-driven model and needed a great deal of effort to get started, but thanks to Foo, who seemed to enjoy the mechanics of it all, the handsome beast chugged around the driveway of Providence with me at the wheel steering its course. Eventually, I felt confident enough to take it on the road. As time passed, I heard that easier to use, gasoline-driven machines were being produced. I had no doubt I would exchange my machine for one of those. Meanwhile, I grew to enjoy and respect my "little monster," and when I took Stephen for his first ride he was ecstatic.

"Granny Mac," he cried with joy. "You are an absolute whiz. No one else's grandmother can drive an automobile!" It was all the encouragement I needed.

When Ernest and Sarah returned in late September of 1902, Stephen moved back to Hamilton House, and I missed him terribly. He had become such a joy to have around, but my sadness was overcome by the new spark I saw in Sarah's eyes. Although I didn't ask, I was convinced she was finally happy with her husband and that perhaps she had taken my words to heart.

I vehemently hoped they would have another child, but it seemed this was not to be in the near future. She and Margaret commiserated together over their failure to conceive as time passed.

On one of the warmest spring mornings in 1903, I was sitting on the side veranda overlooking the rose garden, contemplating how beautiful the roses would be in another month or two when in full bloom. I saw Lum going about his duties. He was a little slower these days, for, like us all, he was getting older.

Suddenly, Foo came through the French doors and stood silently beside me.

"Foo, did you want to go over the dinner menu for tonight?" I asked.

"No, Missee Cap. All under control."

"Oh, good. What a beautiful morning it is, Foo. I don't feel like working ... just enjoying the beauty of my garden."

"Providence very beautiful, Missee Cap."

"Yes, indeed."

He continued to stand there with his hands together and his head slightly bowed.

"Was there something else you wanted, Foo?" I asked.

"Yes, Missee Cap. Something ... else ..."

"What is it, Foo?"

"I decide now to go back to China to my village."

"On a holiday? Why that is wonderful, Foo. You deserve a holiday, even though I don't know how we'll manage without you while you're away ... but we will just have to."

"No holiday, Missee. Go back now for good!"

I looked up at him in amazement. "For good? Oh Foo, you mean ... leave us ...?"

"So sorry, Missee ... but time has come now. Foo getting old. All Chinese go back to the village they were born in so they die there, too."

"Oh, but Foo, you are *not* about to die. You are still young."

"No, Missee Cap. Foo near seventy now ..."

I realized this must be true. Goodness, I was fifty-eight myself, and when Foo first appeared in our lives, he must have been only a few years older than me and a bit younger than Gideon. But where had the years gone? To me, he still seemed the same man he always was, and I could not imagine Providence without him.

But there was absolutely no reasoning with him. I tried desperately to persuade him to stay, telling him that when he became too old to work, we would still look after him, just as we had Angelina.

"There will always be a home here for you at Providence, Foo. You are part of our family."

He nodded. "I know that is true, Missee Cap. But ... my real home is far away. I must return to my village and die with my family."

I had never heard him talk of family, so I was mystified, but I knew of many Chinese who insisted on leaving Canada as they grew old so as to die back in their own villages one day. Nonetheless, his decision stunned me, and I felt extremely sad.

"When have you decided to leave, Foo?" I asked him eventually.

"One week's time," he replied.

"One week! Oh my goodness. So soon, but I shall miss you so much."

"I find other China boy for you, Missee Cap. Young boy, perhaps."

"Perhaps ..." I said vaguely.

"Or maybe, now you have auto machine, you need a man ... what is the name for that?"

"A chauffeur?"

"Yes, some houses in Victoria have man and woman together?"

"Oh, a chauffeur or butler and a housekeeper, you mean?"

"Yes, Missee Cap. You grand lady. Providence grand house. China boy not good enough now."

"Rubbish, Foo," I said. "You are better than any chauffeur, butler or housekeeper put together. You have been everything to us, and always will be."

A small tear trickled down his wrinkled cheek, as he bent his head lower in an effort to avoid my seeing his sadness. I was reminded of another time when I had seen him sobbing under the oak tree, after Caleb died. Yes, Foo was part of our family, but despite my pleadings, I knew his mind was made up. It was a tradition in his culture that he would not ignore.

"Well, Foo, I will insist on one thing. I will help you with your travel plans and pay for your fare. And Mr. Caldwell, I am sure, can arrange for your own money to be transferred to a bank in China."

"Very kind, Missee Cap. But I have saved for the trip, and I prefer to carry my money with me on the journey."

Gosh, he was so stubborn and proud.

"Well, at least allow me to write pre-addressed postcards for you. And you must mail one back to us at each place you stop until you are safely home in China."

He nodded. "That is fine, Missee. Will mail them along the route, but I will be safe."

"Not if someone should discover you are carrying money on you, Foo."

Later, Edward also tried to persuade him, but he insisted on carrying all his belongings, including his money, in his small satchel the day he finally left Providence. His departure left a dark cloud over us all.

None of us could imagine life at Providence without Foo. We watched him walk out of our lives, just as simply and easily as he had walked into Gideon's and my life so many years before. He had been there to share all our joys and our sorrows. He had been, and would always remain, a family member.

That night, as I wrote in my diary of his departure, I felt like part of my heart had been torn away yet again, and I realized once more that nothing is forever. To give love and affection to another human being in this life is simply to know that it is fleeting, and one day it will be taken away from you. I suppose the secret to life is simply to appreciate the times that you have shared and hold them forever in your heart.

*   *   *

Foo's first postcard arrived from Seattle. It simply read, *"Am safe, Foo."* We all breathed a sigh of relief and laughed at his typical brevity of expression.

The second postcard came from San Francisco. "Tomorrow board big ship *Lotus Flower*. Still safe. Foo."

We waited anxiously for postcard number three saying he had arrived in China, but as the weeks and months went by and nothing more arrived, we became seriously worried about his safety. Edward made numerous enquiries about the *Lotus Flower* and did indeed find Foo's name on the passenger list, but there was no proof he had actually boarded the vessel, and when it arrived in Hong Kong, there was no proof that Foo had disembarked. We were all very distraught, imagining all manner of things that could have happened to our beloved Foo.

As months became years, we never did find the answer to the puzzle and we never knew for sure if Foo had indeed reached his village in the Canton area of China to spend his remaining years with his family. That mystique that had always surrounded him at Providence had disappeared with him. But this time, it had left an enormous hole in everyone's heart.

Thankfully, Lum seemed content to spend his remaining years working in the gardens of Providence, but it soon became apparent that we needed to hire more staff, and to this end, both Teddy and Bertie assisted me.

To begin with, we advertised for a chauffeur and housekeeper, as Foo had suggested, and after interviewing numerous couples, many of whom were totally unsuitable, we settled on the Stapletons, an English couple who had worked for a family in New York before deciding to head west and live in Canada.

They were pleasant enough and very hard-working. George Stapleton did all the odd jobs around the house, as well as driving me wherever I wanted to go. He also presented a fine figure of a man as a butler on more formal occasions at Providence. His wife, Alice, was an excellent cook and housekeeper and helped supervise the maids and the running of the house in general. Nonetheless, we all still missed those special little dishes Foo had prepared for us. He had taken all his recipes with him—or maybe there never were any and they had simply all been manufactured from scratch and been stored safely in his head.

When Angelina finally succumbed to a bout of pneumonia the following winter, we were saddened by yet another loss. Although she had been extremely irritating at times, she had been a part of our life at Providence, and it would never be the same without her. The Lodge was now empty, so the Stapletons moved in there from the servants' quarters at Providence, where they had been living.

CHAPTER 31

By 1905, Edward was again visiting Providence on a regular basis, and I enjoyed his company enormously. It was nice, of course, to have the young people around, but Edward and I were more of the same generation, even though he was a decade older than me and was beginning to show his age, but we could share and reminisce about so many things in the past. We would often sit together on the veranda overlooking the garden, talking of days gone by.

"It's a sure sign we must be getting old, Edward," I said on one occasion, as we watched Stephen and Letty, now both eight, organizing little William and John on the lawn in a game of croquet.

"Nonsense, Jane, you will never be old. You are as spry and beautiful as the day Gideon and I first saw you back in '62."

I patted his hand. "How kind you are, dear, but can you not see all the grey hairs? I am well past seventeen now."

"I am blinded by the glints of gold in your beautiful hair."

I turned to look at him. "Why, Edward, how flattering. Tell me, why did you never marry again? Did you ever think about it?"

"Oh many times ..."

"You must have loved your wife, James's mother, very much."

"I suppose I did ... but that was long ago and we were so young."

"Then why did you never find someone else? There have been plenty of ladies who would have loved to marry you." I laughed.

"I'm sure," he said, smiling. He gazed off into the distance, watching the children play. "Trouble was, the only one I would ever have considered was in love with another man."

"Oh Edward, how sad ..."

"No, not really. I was happy for her ... and for him." Something in his tone made me turn and study his expression more earnestly as he added, "He was my best friend, so I would never have made ... overtures to you."

"Dear Edward, you should not—"

"Don't worry, Jane, I'm not about to make a fool of myself, but you must know I have loved you deeply all these many years."

"I did not realize ... although your son hinted at it once to me when he was a child."

"He did?"

"Children are very perceptive. But now it is too late for us. I am content the way things are, and I have always loved you as a friend, but I did love Gideon so very much."

"I know. I know. He was a lucky man."

"No, Edward, I was the lucky one."

We sat in silence for a long time, at peace in our world and with one another.

"You know, something has just occurred to me, Jane," he said, breaking the silence. "Perhaps another generation of our two families will one day fall in love and marry. Look at those two—your grandson and my great-grandaughter ... a McBride and a Caldwell."

"Stephen and Letty! Oh Edward, they are only eight years old!"

"It was just a thought."

We laughed. "You know, Edward, I sometimes think the McBrides are jinxed when it comes to producing children. Poor Margaret has not been able to conceive, and there is no sign yet of a brother or sister for Stephen. As for Bertie, well, he is a confirmed bachelor of sorts, so I fear there will be no children there. But you Caldwells, despite the fact you only had James to start the line going, have been able to produce numerous offspring. James with having Joe, Anna and Kit, and now Joe with his three, Letty, William and John, and Anna in England about to produce her fourth child. It's only Kit who hasn't yet settled down and married ... but I have no doubt he will, one day, up there in the Yukon, where he seems to be making his life. Yes, the Caldwells are definitely very prolific."

He laughed. "So you see, Jane, you should have chosen me back then in '62."

I smiled. "I think I had already been chosen, Edward."

"I think so too, my dear."

We sat there comfortably for a while, just two old friends remembering the past with joy, and imagining the future with hope, as our descendants, Stephen and Letty, played together in the sunshine, quite oblivious to everything and everyone but each other.

EPILOGUE

I thought about what Edward had said for a long time that night before I finally fell into a peaceful sleep.

A union between our two families would have brought such joy to Gideon—and certainly to Edward and me, if it should ever happen in our lifetimes. But, as Sarah often told me, I could not control other people or what would happen in the future.

Still, I wondered if a spark of love would indeed grow between Stephen and Letty in the years to come. I so hoped it would. As the years went by, their friendship remained strong.

But soon there would be other, far more horrifying, things to worry about that would ultimately affect us all.

For, on a distant horizon far away from our peaceful life at Providence on Vancouver Island, the clouds of war were already forming over Europe.

THE END

To be continued in *Legacy* and *Tomorrow*.

ACKNOWLEDGEMENTS

Once again, I wish to thank many people who assisted me with the telling of Sarah and Jane's stories in *Destiny*.

I acknowledge with thanks all the research material others have left concerning the collapse of the Point Ellice Bridge and how the tragedy affected the families living along the Gorge Arm and the whole city of Victoria. Thanks also to the Victoria and Saanich Archives.

And I especially thank the Jacob Hunter Todd family, whose own family history I wrote about in my book *Excelsior* in 1999. Their enormous collection of letters has been especially useful to me while describing the early adventures and later education of Jane and Gideon's twin sons, Bertie and Teddy, and the education of young women at finishing schools. I have taken the liberty of quoting from some of those letters to enhance my story, for which I give full credit to the Todd family.

I am also indebted to many other writers and researchers who covered these periods in history before me and helped with my own research.

And as always, I thank my family and many friends who have supported me for so long. I should add once again that although the historical setting in both *Providence* and *Destiny* is accurate, the house Providence and all my characters are completely fictional, and any resemblance to real people is purely coincidental.

I especially thank the team at Hancock House—Myles, Doreen and Jana—for making this series happen and so much better than I could have ever imagined.

Once again, I acknowledge and am honoured to have placed my fictitious house Providence on the unceded Coast Salish territory of the Lekwungen First Nation people in Victoria, British Columbia.

And last, but by no means least, I am eternally grateful to every reader who buys (and hopefully will review) my books. I could not keep going without you. You are the voices in my head who say "Don't stop!" and for that I thank you all.

ABOUT THE AUTHOR

Valerie Green was born in England and studied journalism, short-story writing and English literature at the Regent Institute of Journalism in London. She aspired to being a writer since she was a child and has always been passionate about history. Before immigrating to Canada in 1968, Valerie's employment included a short stint at the War Office for MI5, as well as legal secretarial work and freelance writing. Her writing career is  extensive and includes writing a weekly history column for the *Saanich News* for nineteen years, a monthly column for the Seaside Times in Sidney, BC, for ten years, articles for the Victoria Times Colonist, as well as authoring more than twenty books on local and regional history, mysteries and social issues. Now semi-retired, Valerie reviews books for Brititsh Columbia Reviews and freelances for newspapers and magazines.

She lives with her husband in Saanich, BC, on Vancouver Island.

Visit her website at www.valeriegreenauthor.com or connect with her at hello@valeriegreenauthor.com

THE McBRIDE CHRONICLES

This four-book series spans through six generations of two families, from the 1840s to present day. Strong women characters who overcome incredible odds are included in each of the four books, intertwined with real historical events through British Columbia and Canada.

Hancock House Publishers
19313 0 Ave, Surrey, BC V3Z 9R9
www.hancockhouse.com
sales@hancockhouse.com
1-800-938-1114

Made in the USA
Monee, IL
20 September 2023